"Wow! Kara Lennox's BLOND JUSTICE series has it all—smart, determined heroines, ya-gotta-love-'em macho heroes, taut suspense and romance that will steam your glasses while it melts your heart. Each book is a winner; together they're pure magic."
—*USA TODAY* bestselling author
Merline Lovelace

Dear Reader,

There's almost nothing more stressful than a wedding. Sonya Patterson has the added stress of a mom in the hospital, a con-man groom after her millions, a reporter hunting for scandal, and the man she's loved and hated her whole life suddenly becoming more than her dutiful bodyguard.

I had a lot of fun wrapping up the BLOND JUSTICE series. If you've enjoyed watching The Blondes get the best of slippery con man Marvin Carter, you'll be delighted with their brand of ultimate justice. But I hope you'll also take pleasure in watching Sonya and John-Michael work through barriers of wealth, social class and a painful history to reach the happy ending they deserve.

Please let me know what you think! I love hearing from readers. Visit me at www.karalennox.com or write me at karalennox@yahoo.com.

All my best,

Kara Lennox

OUT OF TOWN
BRIDE
Kara Lennox

HARLEQUIN®

TORONTO • NEW YORK • LONDON
AMSTERDAM • PARIS • SYDNEY • HAMBURG
STOCKHOLM • ATHENS • TOKYO • MILAN • MADRID
PRAGUE • WARSAW • BUDAPEST • AUCKLAND

ISBN 0-373-75097-8

OUT OF TOWN BRIDE

Copyright © 2005 by Karen Leabo.

This edition published by arrangement with Harlequin Books S.A.

® and TM are trademarks of the publisher. Trademarks indicated with ® are registered in the United States Patent and Trademark Office, the Canadian Trade Marks Office and in other countries.

www.eHarlequin.com

Printed in U.S.A.

For the Thursday Lunch-'n-Starbucks crowd—
Victoria Chancellor, Judy Christenberry, Kay Dykes,
Tammy Hilz and Rebecca Russell. Y'all keep me sane.

Books by Kara Lennox

HARLEQUIN AMERICAN ROMANCE

934—VIXEN IN DISGUISE*
942—PLAIN JANE'S PLAN*
951—SASSY CINDERELLA*
974—FORTUNE'S TWINS
990—THE MILLIONAIRE NEXT DOOR
1052—THE FORGOTTEN COWBOY
1068—HOMETOWN HONEY†
1081—DOWNTOWN DEBUTANTE†

*How To Marry a Hardison
†Blond Justice

Prologue

Airplane seats were way too small and too crowded together. Sonya Patterson had never thought much about it before, since she'd always flown first class in the past. But this was a last-minute ticket on a no-first-class kind of plane.

She'd also never flown on a commercial airline with her bodyguard, which might explain her current claustrophobia. John-Michael McPhee was a broad-shouldered, well-muscled man, and Sonya was squashed between him and a hyperactive seven-year-old whose mother was fast asleep in the row behind them.

She could smell the leather of McPhee's bomber jacket. He'd had that jacket for years, and every time Sonya saw him in it, her stupid heart gave a little leap. She hated herself for letting him affect her that way. Didn't most women get over their teenage crushes by the time they were pushing thirty?

"I didn't know you were a nervous flyer," McPhee said, brushing his index finger over her left hand. Sonya realized she was clutching her armrests as if the plane were about to crash.

What would he think, she wondered, if she blurted out that it wasn't the flying that made her nervous, it was being so close to him? Her mother would not approve of Sonya's messy feelings where McPhee was concerned.

Her mother. Sonya's heart ached at the thought of her vibrant mother lying in a hospital bed hooked up to machines. Muffy Lockridge Patterson was one of those women who never stopped running all day, every day, at full throttle with a to-do list a mile long. Over the years Sonya had often encouraged her mother to slow down, relax and cut back on the rich foods. But Muffy seldom took advice from anyone.

Sonya consciously loosened her grip on the armrests when McPhee nudged her again.

"She'll be okay," he said softly. "She was in stable condition when I left, and Tootsie was with her."

"Tootsie? Is that supposed to comfort me?" Tootsie Milford, Muffy's best friend since boarding school, was a consummate snob who never did a kindness for anyone unless she thought she could get something out of it—usually attention.

Sonya said little else to McPhee during the short flight, and he returned the favor. It was only after the limo picked them up at Hobby Airport that they spoke openly, safe from curious eavesdroppers.

"Do you want to go home first?" McPhee asked.

"No, of course not. Tim," she said, addressing the chauffeur, "let's go straight to the hospital, please."

Tim hit the gas as Sonya fastened her seat belt. McPhee, as usual, didn't bother. Sonya tried her best to ignore him. She rooted through her suede bag for her compact and busied herself powdering her nose and refreshing her lipstick. Other people might consider her vain, worrying about her appearance during a crisis. But grooming rituals had always given her comfort. That was something she and her mother shared. The world might be crashing down around her ears, but that didn't mean she had to take it with a shiny nose and flyaway hair.

"Are you going to tell me what you were doing in New Orleans with your 'sorority sister'?" McPhee asked, apparently unwilling to be ignored.

So, he hadn't bought her cover story. But she'd had to come up with something quickly when McPhee had tracked her down hundreds of miles away from where she was supposed to be. She'd already been caught in a bald-faced lie—for weeks she'd been telling her mother she was at a spa in Dallas, working out her prewedding jitters.

"I was shopping in New Orleans for my trousseau," she tried again. "Brenna's a fashion consultant."

McPhee laughed out loud at that one. "Lord help us if you start dressing like *her.*"

All right, so Brenna was a little avant-garde with her spiky hair, miniskirts and platform shoes.

"Anyway," McPhee continued, "why would a fashion consultant be wanted by the FBI? Come on, Sonya, who is she? And don't tell me she's an old friend. I know all your old friends."

"You think you know *everything* about me, don't you? Well, you don't. I met Brenna at the spa."

"I checked with Elizabeth Arden. You haven't been there in over three years."

"I went to a different spa this time." The lies were stacking up—and none of them were flying with McPhee.

He didn't respond, merely stared her down with those incongruously dark-brown eyes. His eyes had always fascinated her, so dark when his hair was blond, and so blasted knowing, as if he could see straight to her most intimate thoughts.

She resisted the urge to squirm under his gaze. She was an adult, she reminded herself. "I have private reasons for my trip to New Orleans, and they don't concern you."

"Very well, Miss Patterson," he said in his Jeeves-the-butler voice. "Forgive me for overstepping my bounds."

She hated it when he accused her of acting like mistress of the manor. *She* wasn't the class-conscious one around here, after all. In fact, she'd once tried to erase the social and financial barriers that separated them. McPhee was the one who had erected most of those barriers, making them more unbreakable than a twenty-foot concrete wall.

"What are you going to do about the wedding?" McPhee asked, abruptly changing tacks. "It's only two months away."

Sonya felt a hot flush at the mention of the wedding. Oh, Lord, she should have called it off a long time ago. "We'll consider the wedding on hold until we have an idea when my mother will recover."

"I think that's wise."

"You sound almost pleased. I thought you were looking forward to being unemployed." Muffy had agreed that, much as it pained her, McPhee's services would no longer be needed after Sonya was married.

"I don't plan to be unemployed," McPhee said curtly. "You might want to talk to June. She'll have to find a way to announce the wedding postponement without raising any alarms." June was her mother's secretary, who always dealt with anything having to do with the media.

"Has the press been nosing around?" Sonya asked.

"June issued a statement that Mrs. Patterson was going in for routine tests. But there's been one persistent magazine reporter who isn't buying it."

"Let me guess. Leslie Frazier?"

"That's the one."

Ugh. Leslie Frazier had a nose for scandal, and she worked for *Houston Living,* a gossipy society magazine. If she got wind of Sonya's disappearing act, she'd have a field day. And when she found out the truth—that the marriage would never take place at all, followed by the truth about her purported fiancé, Marvin Carter III—she would turn Sonya into a laughingstock.

Sonya knew she couldn't stop the real story from coming out eventually. It was only a matter of time. But she wished she could have some control over how and when the news broke.

The truth was, Marvin Carter III was a con man with multiple "fiancées." Weeks earlier, Marvin had disappeared from Sonya's life, along with her jewelry, her furs and all her money.

Yet she hadn't found the courage to tell her mother she'd been jilted and fleeced, and wedding plans continued like a runaway train.

Chapter One

Two weeks later John-Michael McPhee watched Sonya silently for a few moments. She sat at her mother's bedside, holding Muffy's limp hand, head bowed. Her artfully highlighted blond hair, which she usually kept pinned up in some elaborate arrangement, had long ago fallen from its confines and now hung in shimmering waves to her shoulders, reminding him of when she was a teenager.

At first, it had seemed that Muffy would recover quickly from her heart attack. She'd been doing so well, in fact, that Sonya had felt it was okay to leave town for a couple of days to help her mysterious new friend, Brenna, out of a jam up in Dallas. But as soon as Sonya had returned, Muffy had undergone bypass surgery, and her recovery hadn't gone well. She'd contracted a persistent infection that had kept her in Intensive Care.

John-Michael hadn't seen Sonya so devastated since her father's death when she was ten. Back then, the transformation of that bright, sunny chatterbox to the thin, solemn, pale little wraith floating about the estate had nearly broken his teenage heart, and he'd tried everything in his power to make her happy again.

Now, however, there wasn't much he could do; she wasn't a child to be distracted—especially not by him. He was one of her least favorite people these days.

He cleared his throat. Sonya looked over at him, for once open and vulnerable. She hadn't expressed that much feeling in years—not around him, anyway.

"You really should go home and get some sleep," John-Michael said. Sonya had been sitting by Muffy's bedside for almost twenty-four hours.

"But she woke up and spoke to me a few minutes ago. She said she was…sorry for getting sick so close to my wedding." Sonya's eyes filled with tears. "That was the first thing she wanted to say to me."

John-Michael felt the urge to put his arms around Sonya and comfort her. He knew she felt guilty for being gone when her mother was suddenly struck ill, and for not returning his urgent calls. And there was no one else she could turn to for comfort. Muffy and Sonya had no other family. They had no siblings in either generation.

But Sonya would not welcome comfort from him.

Her fiancé should be with her now, John-Michael thought with a surge of anger. But Marvin, the insensitive lout, was halfway around the globe and apparently couldn't be bothered.

"Your mother wouldn't want you to wear yourself to a frazzle," John-Michael said.

"I'm staying," she said stubbornly. "If you're tired, go on home. I'll be fine."

John-Michael gritted his teeth. For ten years he'd hovered over Sonya, knowing her whereabouts at all times. He'd followed her at a discreet distance whenever she dated; he'd slept in his car outside strange houses when she'd elected to spend the night away from home. He'd sat in doctors' waiting rooms and outside college classrooms, watching as she lived her life, wondering if he would ever get to live his.

Sonya hadn't needed a bodyguard. She'd never been threatened or stalked, and she was in no more danger than any other wealthy young woman. But Muffy couldn't bear to take chances with her only daughter, not after her husband had been kidnapped and killed, targeted due to his wealth. The murderers were safely in prison, but Muffy worried it could happen again.

It wasn't likely John-Michael would abandon Sonya now, when Muffy was lying in Intensive Care.

Instead, he resumed his vigil on a padded bench in the ICU waiting area, a bench he'd been warming on and off since the day he brought Sonya here from New Orleans.

Thirty minutes later, Sonya emerged from the ICU. "The nurses kicked me out. I guess I've been trying their patience, abusing their visitors' rules."

"They probably just want you to get some sleep."

She eyed the lumpy bench he was parked on. "I could sleep there."

"Sonya…"

"Oh, all right. I guess it wouldn't hurt for me to catch a couple of hours' sleep at home. The nurses have my cell number. They promised to call if there's any change." She gave him a rare, sympathetic look. "You look bushed. You don't really have to stay here with me all the time."

"Marvin's the one who should be with you."

She glanced away, a sure sign she was about to tell a lie. "I told you, he's somewhere in China right now. I can't get hold of him."

"Can't you call his company?" John-Michael said as they walked toward the elevator. "Surely they know how to reach him. And there are satellite phones, you know."

"He's working on an important deal, and I don't want to worry him unnecessarily. He calls me every few days. I'll let him know the situation next time he calls."

John-Michael sure wished he knew what was going on with her. He'd never known Sonya to be so secretive—or to tell so many lies. He and Sonya had had their differences, sure, but she'd always been able to trust him. He'd never told Muffy about those frat parties she used to attend that were little more than drunken orgies. Or about the time he'd had to rush Sonya's best friend, Cissy Trask, to the hospital when she'd had a miscarriage. No one but he and Sonya had known she was pregnant, and no one ever would.

Why now had Sonya decided he couldn't be trusted?

Once they reached the Patterson estate, Sonya disappeared without a word up the curved staircase, her delicate heels noiseless on the Chinese silk carpeting.

John-Michael retreated to his own quarters, a small apartment above the five-car garage. But he was too keyed up to sleep. Instead, he pulled on a pair of gym shorts.

The Patterson estate had its own mini health club, with state-of-the-art exercise equipment, an indoor lap pool, wet and dry saunas and whirlpool.

Foregoing the fancier equipment, John-Michael went a few rounds with a punching bag.

As he moved through a series of jabs and kicks, he thought about the easy friendship he and Sonya had enjoyed when they were kids. Though he was only the gardener's son and Sonya was five years his junior, she'd been his sidekick, his little pest, always trailing after him, wanting to hang out with him and his friends. And sometimes he'd let her slum with him. He'd shown her how to work on his motorcycle and, at Muffy's insistence, how to handle the gun Sonya now kept in her nightstand.

When Muffy decided Sonya needed a bodyguard. John-Michael was the logical choice. He'd just graduated from the police academy, planning a career in law enforcement. Muffy offered him a higher salary than any of the local police departments paid, *and* she'd promised to send him to an elite bodyguard-training school. He'd cheerfully accepted, never realizing he was putting a noose around his own neck.

Muffy had a secondary motive for hiring John-Michael. She'd needed him close at hand to handle any "difficulties" that came up with Jock, her gardener—who happened to be John-Michael's father.

The job had gone okay until one night when Sonya attended her first sorority party. John-Michael had gone with her, lurking in the shadows like always, watching as she tried to assert her independence by getting drunk on margaritas. He'd pulled her away from the party before things had gone too far.

She'd been spitting angry with him at first, spouting off about how she was an adult, it was a free world, she would have her mother fire him. Then, when they'd reached the car, she'd surprised the hell out of him by throwing her arms around his neck and pressing her lush body up against his. "I really am a bad girl, aren't I?" Before he could answer, before he'd been able to think, she'd clamped her sweet little mouth over his.

His body had sprung to life, and for the first time he'd realized that his charge was no longer a child. She had a woman's body, a woman's moves….

After thirty seconds of hot kisses and body rubbing, he'd pulled himself together and gently pushed her away.

"What?" she'd objected, loudly enough to wake the whole neighborhood. "Don't tell me you don't want me. You do. I could feel it."

Dear God. At that moment he'd seen the utter folly of what he'd done, what he'd been *about* to do. Having sex with his charge, the girl he was supposed to be protecting, would be the grossest sort of irresponsibility he could imagine, not to mention a very short path to losing his job.

The only way to deal with this situation, he'd decided, was to end it in a way that was harsh and final, so it would never happen again. So he would never be tempted again.

He gave his punching bag a series of savage jabs as he remembered how difficult it had been to be cruel to her.

He'd forced himself to laugh at her. "You don't actually imagine I would be interested in a spoiled little brat like you," he'd said, deliberately filling his voice with derision.

The insult had cut, as it was meant to do. Her eyes filled with tears. "You kissed me back," she accused.

"I'm a man," he said harshly. "I have hormones. But I also have a brain, thank God, and I'm not stupid enough to get it on with Muffy Patterson's daughter."

"She would never know," Sonya said in a last-ditch effort to salvage the situation. And it almost worked. Seeing her standing there, more sober now than drunk, her blond hair mussed, her lips full from kissing, he'd almost grabbed her and kissed her again. And he wouldn't have stopped with kissing.

Savagely he turned his back on her and opened the passenger door of her BMW—her high school graduation present from Muffy. "Get in the car. You're embarrassing yourself."

"Do you have a girlfriend?" she asked, sounding devastated at the thought.

"That's none of your business." He hoped she would think that meant yes.

"I've never seen you with a girl."

"No girlfriend of mine is going to watch while a child orders me around."

He hadn't had a girlfriend. When would he have had time to find one? He'd spent every hour either watching over Sonya or dealing with the disasters his father created. But his ploy had worked. Sonya didn't say another word. And she never again tested her feminine wiles on him.

Back in the present, he took one final swing at the bag. He was out of breath and dripping with sweat, more so than the easy workout should have caused. Time hadn't lessened the intensity of his memories one bit.

Unfortunately, his formerly easygoing friendship with Sonya had been a casualty of that ill-begotten evening. She'd never forgotten, or forgiven, his rejection. For almost ten years, he'd had to endure her coldness and hide the desire he felt for her, a desire that had only grown fiercer as she'd matured into an intriguing woman.

He'd tried to resign, and Sonya had tried to fire him—numerous times. But gradually, John-Michael had come to understand the complex dynamics of his job. If he wasn't employed in a position that kept him constantly on hand to handle Jock, then Jock would have to go.

And to send Jock away from the Patterson estate, the only home he'd ever known, would kill him.

SONYA HADN'T REALIZED how tired she was. When next she woke, it was dark outside. She checked her clock and was horrified to discover it was after two in the morning.

Her first thought was that they'd been protecting her from bad news—"they" being John-Michael; Tim, the chauffeur; June, the secretary; and possibly Matilda, the housekeeper. Muffy's staff had always sheltered Sonya from all unpleasantries.

She sat up, rubbed the sleep from her eyes and

switched on a lamp. Her cell phone was right there next to her, with no messages. Grateful that she'd had the foresight to put the ICU's phone number into her cell's memory, she dialed.

"Your mother is actually doing much better," the night nurse told her. "The new antibiotic therapy is working. She's been drifting in and out of sleep, but she did wake up long enough to drink some water. She asked about you."

Sonya was already on her feet. "I'll be there in twenty minutes."

"No, you don't have to do that," the nurse said firmly. "I asked your mother if she wanted me to call you, and she said no, absolutely not, that you needed your sleep."

That sounded like Muffy, Sonya thought with a frown. The benevolent dictator, issuing orders from her sick bed.

"She's fine, really," the nurse insisted. "In fact, they'll probably move her out of ICU tomorrow."

That news brought a flood of relief. Sonya hesitated, then decided it probably would serve no good to rush to the hospital in the middle of the night if Muffy was sleeping and in no immediate danger. "If she wakes again, tell her I'll be there first thing in the morning," she said. "Unless she needs me sooner."

After the call, Sonya felt better, but there was no way she was going back to sleep. She was, in fact, hungry. She'd hardly eaten a bite since Muff's surgery several days ago. She threw on a robe and wandered downstairs to the enormous, restaurant-grade kitchen, certain there would be several tasty dishes in the fridge. That was something she could always count on.

As she entered the huge white-tile-and-chrome room, she flipped on a light so bright it hurt her eyes. The stainless steel appliances gleamed with a recent polish, and the room smelled faintly of fresh-baked bread. As top dog among Houston society mavens, Muffy often gave elaborate dinner parties, for which she had Eric, a Cordon-Bleu-trained chef, prepare gourmet delights that were sure to be written up on the society page *and* in the food section. And for every day, they had Eric's mother, Matilda, a traditional Southern cook down to her bones.

The glass-fronted refrigerator was crammed with dozens of ceramic storage dishes, neatly stacked and labeled with the contents and the throwaway date. Sonya perused the labels, wrinkling her nose. She was not in the mood for Eric's dill-crusted sea bass with Parmesan cream sauce, or marmalade-glazed pork medallions and shiitake mushrooms. Then she spotted something that appealed to her—Matilda's macaroni and cheese. Pure comfort food and a guilty indulgence she and her mother sometimes ate when they were dining alone.

She pulled it out and stuck it in the microwave.

Slowly she realized she was no longer alone in the room. John-Michael stood in the doorway, looking adorably rumpled in gym shorts and an old T-shirt bearing the logo of Close Protection, Inc., where he'd gotten his bodyguard training.

"Are you okay?" he asked. He had this uncanny ability to know whenever she stirred at night. He always noticed when lights went on or if anyone made the slightest noise. She wondered if he ever slept or if he sat up all night, ever vigilant.

"I got hungry," she answered. "I don't think that's any reason to call out the National Guard." She immediately felt guilty for sniping at him, though. "Sorry. It's been a rough few days. You want some macaroni and cheese?"

"Sure." He went to the fridge and poured himself some milk. Without asking, he pulled out a bottle of her favorite cherry-flavored mineral water, uncapped it and set it out for her.

He knew her so well, probably better than her own mother did. And it irked her. She'd actually been looking forward to escaping his knowing eyes once she was married. Now that wasn't going to happen. She saw herself in twenty years, thirty years, fifty, still single, still living in Muffy's house, McPhee still watching over her with his eagle eyes. Still waiting for those few moments when he could escape her and go to whatever girlfriend he would undoubtedly have. He'd probably still be shadowing her every move when they were both in the nursing home. Gawd, what a depressing thought.

"I called the hospital," she said. "Mother's doing better. She drank some water and told the nurses not to call me."

"Already back to her bossy self, huh?" But McPhee's smile was of pure relief. She didn't blame him. Muffy was a kind employer, if a tad inflexible. She paid her staff far more than the going rate to inspire their loyalty, and it worked.

But McPhee was genuinely fond of Muffy, too. As hard as Sonya was on McPhee, she knew he wasn't completely self-serving.

When the microwave dinged, Sonya took out the dish and scooped generous portions onto white, bone-china plates with gold rims, the only kind Muffy would have in her house. She had a thing against plastic and thought stoneware was almost as bad. Sonya and McPhee sat at the kitchen table and ate with mono-grammed sterling forks.

"Mmm, I love this stuff," McPhee said.

"We better enjoy it while we can. I imagine we'll see some changes around here when Muffy gets home. Matilda and Eric will have to prepare heart-healthy meals."

"Matilda will screech like a banshee over that," McPhee said.

"She'll have to get used to it. I've been telling Mother for years that her diet is impossibly unhealthy. She'll have to listen to me now."

"Muffy never listens to anyone."

Sonya sighed. "I know. She has her ideas about the way things should be, and nothing's going to change them." Certainly not Sonya, whose opinions Muffy had always considered superfluous. Muffy knew what was best, and that was that.

"Maybe if we join forces?" McPhee suggested. "Two against one."

Sonya laughed harshly. "That would be a first. We haven't agreed on anything since…well, since we were children."

Since that night at the sorority party, she'd almost said. Sonya's skin prickled at the memory, still vivid af-ter all these years.

"I think if we present a united front," McPhee said, "Muffy will *have* to pay attention."

"Since when do you call her Muffy, anyway?"

He shrugged. "I don't, not to her face. Just to you."

"To irritate me."

He didn't deny it, just flashed that inscrutable half smile of his that drove her crazy. "Don't worry, you'll be rid of me soon. You haven't officially postponed the wedding, have you?"

"No." Another wave of guilt washed over her. But she could hardly announce she was going to call off the wedding when Muffy was still so ill. "Mother said to wait and see how she did after the surgery. Are you counting the days?"

"Only forty-nine days to go."

She tried to hide her surprise. She'd only been kidding about counting the days. Was he that unhappy? He often aggravated her, but she wasn't miserable with their arrangement. "Just what are you planning to do with your newfound freedom? I assume Muffy has another job for you."

McPhee shook his head. "I've already applied and been accepted at the Harris County Sheriff's Department."

This was news to Sonya, and it shook her to the core. She had a hard time visualizing this house, this estate, without John-Michael as a constant fixture. "What about your dad?"

"Dad's on the wagon."

"Yes, but for how long?"

McPhee pushed his plate away without finishing,

alerting Sonya to the fact that she'd ticked him off. He always cleaned his plate. "I've spent ten years as a virtual prisoner," he said, "to my father, to Muffy and to you. That's long enough. If my father does something crazy and gets himself fired, I'll deal with it. But I'm not going to let the fear of that stop me from living. Not anymore."

Sonya hadn't heard much past the word "prisoner." "If conditions are so wretched here, why didn't you quit?" she challenged him.

"You don't think I've tried? But your mother made it pretty clear. If I left, Jock had to go, too. I couldn't do that to him. He has nowhere else to go."

"How are things different now?"

"Your mother is being a bit more flexible, now that your future is secured and my dad's behaving himself. I think he finally understands the consequences if he messes up again. Maybe he won't this time."

Sonya wanted to believe that Jock McPhee's drinking days were over, but she found it difficult. She recalled all too well the sort of mayhem that ensued when Jock went on a bender. Once he'd driven the riding lawnmower right through the living room window and into the middle of one of Muffy's tea parties. Another time he'd gotten a chainsaw and lopped off half of an ancient oak tree because he was tired of fishing its leaves out of the pool; he'd nearly chopped off one of his arms, as well.

Muffy should have fired Jock long ago, but she had such a soft heart she couldn't do it. Besides, when Jock was sober, he was the best gardener in all of Houston and a very nice person. Sonya, as well, had always had a soft spot for Jock. He'd been especially kind to her when she was grieving over her father's death.

So had McPhee. The teenage boy who'd had no use for a ten-year-old girl had suddenly stopped tormenting her. He'd started showing her small kindnesses, offering to drive her to visit friends if Tim was busy, playing volleyball with her in the pool.

That was when she'd first fallen in love with him.

Oh, hell, she didn't want to think about that now. "Well, I wish you luck in your new career. And I'm sorry we've made your life so unpleasant."

"No, you're not," he said with a little grin. "You did it on purpose. You've resented me watching your every move as much as I've resented having to play nursemaid to a spoiled debutante."

Sonya laid down her fork. "Boy, you're really taking the gloves off."

"I feel a certain recklessness, knowing I'll soon be free."

"Now is not the time for me to find out you hate me," she said. "I have enough to deal with."

"I don't hate you."

"You just think I'm spoiled."

"Anyone who doesn't have to work for a living is spoiled. It's not your fault you were born with so much money."

Sonya wanted to continue the argument. Unfortunately, she knew he was right. She'd never wanted for anything in her life, something she'd taken for granted. Did that make her spoiled?

Without a good comeback, she returned her attention to her macaroni and cheese, hoping he would go away.

He did. He rinsed his plate, put it in the dishwasher and left the kitchen without another word.

Sonya felt guilty, though she didn't know why. McPhee was such a thorn in her side, always lurking, nosy about everything she did, every person she saw. But she'd known for a long time that being her body-guard wasn't his dream job. It was boring. He'd never once had to protect her from anything more threatening than a pushy salesman. Yet he'd tried to make the best of it.

What a relief it would be for both of them, she sup-posed, if he went away. Once her mother found out So-nya wasn't getting married, she would try to keep McPhee on the payroll. But she had a feeling his mind was made up. This time, he was really going, really moving out of her life.

A noise at the kitchen door startled Sonya. The Pat-terson estate had security up the wazoo. At night the gates were locked up tight, and electronic sensors around the perimeter fence would detect any intruder. But Sonya had inherited some of her mother's paranoia, she supposed. Whenever she heard a strange noise at night, or even if a stranger looked at her funny, she mentally reviewed escape routes and the location of the nearest weapons for self-defense.

The sound at the door came again, and then the door opened. Sonya tensed, then relaxed when she recog-nized the nocturnal visitor. It was just Jock McPhee, John-Michael's father, who was harmless as a baby bird so long as he hadn't been drinking. And even drunk, he wasn't mean, just a bit reckless.

"Hello, Jock," Sonya said, alert for any sign that the gardener had been drinking. Jock was probably no more than five-ten, small and wiry. There was some resemblance to John-Michael in the lean face and the shape of his jaw, but that was where the resemblance ended. His coarse hair, once a dark brown, was salt-and-pepper, and it stood out from his head in unruly tufts, as if he'd just gotten out of bed. His cheeks bore a day-old, silvery beard, and his front teeth were slightly crooked, though still a bright white.

His most startling feature was his eyes, a vibrant sea blue. They hadn't faded with age. And in this instance, they were clear and alert. No sign that he'd fallen off the wagon. His work pants were old and faded, but clean, held up by his trademark rainbow suspenders.

"Hello, Miss Sonya," he said with a tentative smile. He spoke with the faint trace of an Irish cadence, a legacy from his home country. "I couldn't sleep, and I saw the light. I hope you don't mind the intrusion."

"Of course I don't mind. Would you like some macaroni and cheese?"

He shook his head. "I'm not very hungry these days. I just can't seem to settle down since they carted Miss Muffy to the hospital. Nothing bad's happened, has it?"

Sonya's heart went out to the man. He'd lived on the Patterson estate since he was a baby, when his mother came here to work as a cook. He and Muffy had grown up together. They often fought like a couple of bulldogs over what should be planted and where. Muffy had some old, decrepit camellia bushes that she absolutely refused to let Jock replace or even prune, though they were overgrown and past their prime, and they argued about those silly bushes on a monthly basis. But Sonya knew there was a deep, mutual fondness between the two. No one had given Jock much thought the past couple of days, but he was probably devastated over her mother's health crisis.

"My mother is doing better," Sonya said. "I just heard from the hospital. They might even move her out of Intensive Care tomorrow."

"Oh, praise the heavens," Jock said, sinking into a kitchen chair. "I've been just sick with worry. Is there anything I can do? Oh, of course there isn't, but that's what everybody asks at a time like this."

"I'm sure my mother would appreciate your kind thoughts and prayers," Sonya said gently.

"Do you think—would it be all right if I visited her at the hospital? I wouldn't stay long. I could bring her a few blooms from the greenhouse."

"She would love to see you, I'm sure. I'll let you know as soon as she's allowed visitors."

"Thank you, Miss Sonya. I imagine this has put a kink in your wedding plans."

"We may have to delay the ceremony," she confirmed. Every time she said it, she felt relieved. When would it be appropriate for her to call the church and give up the date she'd selected, January eighth? Once the wedding was no longer scheduled, it would be easy just to never reschedule. Then it would be easier still to convince her mother she'd changed her mind about tying the knot with Marvin. Maybe she would never have to tell Muffy what a fool she'd been, allowing Marvin to fleece her. The whole subject of Marvin could just quietly disappear.

"I was looking forward to making your wedding bouquet myself," Jock said quietly. "I know you've hired a big fancy florist to do all the arrangements, but I was hoping…well, I have some of the most beautiful roses you've ever seen in the greenhouse."

"Why, Jock, I'd be honored to have you do that for me." She knew he was up to the task. He often put together fantastic arrangements for the house. "Don't pick out the blooms just yet," she added hastily. "But whenever I do get married, I definitely want you to do my bouquet."

He seemed pleased to hear her say that, and he offered her a warm smile. "Thank you, Miss Sonya. You and your mother have always been so good to me, even in bad times."

"Your son tells me the bad times are over," she said.

"I'm working real hard," Jock confirmed. "I'm in AA. In fact, I thought I'd head out to a meeting right now."

"Do they have meetings at this time of the night?"

"Just about any time you need one, you can find it. And I need one. This thing with your mother—well, if a man can't drink when someone he cares for is at death's door, when *can* he drink?"

Sonya wasn't used to Jock speaking so freely about his drinking problem, but she supposed it was a good sign that maybe he really had made lasting changes in his life.

"Don't let me keep you," she said. "And I'm proud of you. I know it can't be easy, changing the habits of a lifetime."

"There are some habits you can change," he said. "And some you can't." With that cryptic comment, he tipped an imaginary hat and departed.

Chapter Two

John-Michael quickly noted that Sonya wasn't speaking to him as they rode in the limousine toward the hospital the following morning.

"I might have been out of line," he ventured, "calling you spoiled."

"Stuff it."

Okay. She was under stress and he wasn't helping her any. She'd been acting hinky since she'd returned from her mysterious road trip.

"Were you having an affair?" John-Michael asked. "Is that what New Orleans was about?"

"Yes. With Brenna," she added, deadpan. "Thank goodness my secret is finally out in the open."

Tim, who wasn't supposed to be listening, snorted from the front seat.

"I just can't imagine what would have drawn you to some of the places you visited over the past few weeks," John-Michael continued. "Dallas makes sense. But Cottonwood, Texas? And then, some sleazy motel in Smoky Bayou, Louisiana?"

Cottonwood was where Cindy Rheems, another of Marvin's victims, lived. Smoky Bayou was one of the many stops they'd made as they'd tracked Marvin across two states, always a step behind him. "Will you please just let it drop?"

"I'm responsible for your safety, which means I need to know what's going on in your life."

"I hereby absolve you of your responsibility."

They'd been through this conversation, or ones very similar, countless times since he'd taken the job as her bodyguard.

When they reached the hospital, rather than following standard procedure for entering a public building, Sonya charged out of the limousine toward the front canopy of Harris County Medical Center without waiting for John-Michael to check things out and then escort her. Usually there was no need for extreme security. Unfortunately, today wasn't usual.

A reporter with a tape recorder appeared out of nowhere heading Sonya off before she could get to the door.

"Miss Patterson, Leslie Frazier from *Houston Living* magazine. Is your mother all right?"

"Yes, my mother is fine," Sonya said smoothly, a polite smile pasted on.

"A source close to the situation says your mother is in Intensive Care, that she's had a heart attack."

John-Michael was about to jump in and rescue his charge, but she handled the situation just fine.

"She's undergoing tests," Sonya said firmly. "I have no further comments."

The reporter, seeing John-Michael, looked at him hopefully, but he wouldn't make eye contact, and the firm set of his mouth apparently dissuaded the perky redhead from asking any further questions.

"You shouldn't go charging ahead of me like that," John-Michael said when they were out of the reporter's earshot.

"You've been reading your own press," Sonya said, sounding annoyed. "She was a five-foot-two bubble-head who probably doesn't weigh a hundred pounds soaking wet. I wasn't in any danger."

"She could have been someone more dangerous."

"McPhee, in all the years you've been guarding me, has anyone ever threatened me?"

"No," he admitted.

"The danger is all in my mother's head. And you've bought into it. Get over yourself." She switched off her cell phone as they entered the building, reminding him to do the same.

They discovered that Muffy was no longer in the In-tensive Care Unit. She'd been moved to a regular room. When they finally located her, she was sitting up in bed, her eyes open, the TV on, though John-Michael didn't think she was actually watching the show. She wasn't exactly a Jerry Springer fan. Though she was still hooked up to an IV and oxygen, she looked about 500 percent less scary than yesterday.

"Mother?"

Muffy looked over and managed a faint smile. "So-nya. And John-Michael, how nice."

He walked up to the bed and squeezed her hand.

"Mrs. Patterson. You must be feeling better. You look great."

"Liar. I must…look like…day-old…paté de foie gras." Her speech was labored, and it pained John-Michael to see her laid so low. But at least she was awake, and seemingly alert.

"Mother, don't try to talk," Sonya said.

"I want…to talk. I have to thank…John-Michael. I should have said something…long ago."

"Thank him for what?"

"For making me go…to the hospital. I thought it was…indigestion. And for finding my girl…and bringing her home."

Sonya flicked a curious glance toward John-Michael. "You did that? Brought her to the E.R.? How come no one told me?"

"It was a group effort," John-Michael said modestly.

"Well, thank you," Sonya said. "You probably saved her life."

He shrugged. He didn't consider himself a hero. He'd done what anyone would do. Anyway, having Sonya's gratitude felt alien. He was much more comfortable when she was mad at him.

Sonya returned her attention to her mother, brushing her hand lightly against Muffy's cheek. "I'm sorry I wasn't here when you got sick." She'd already apologized several times, but she felt compelled to repeat herself.

"I know, pumpkin. Is Marvin here?"

"He's still in China. I can't get hold of him." She said this quickly, as if she'd rehearsed the answer over and over. And her eyes flickered up and to the right. John-Michael had studied neuro-linguistic programming as part of his criminology curriculum. Sonya was lying, or at least not telling the whole truth about Marvin's whereabouts. John-Michael wished he could get to the bottom of this mystery, but he didn't want to press Sonya when she was still so worried about her mother.

"How are the wedding plans coming?" Muffy said to Sonya.

"I've put the wedding on hold," Sonya said firmly. "We're not going to focus on anything for a while except getting you well."

"You can't postpone it," Muffy said, her voice suddenly stronger. "We'll lose our date at the country club!"

"Mother, don't worry about it. I promise it will be fine. We'll work it out. I want you to focus on getting better."

"It's not for two months," Muffy persisted. "I'll be fine by then."

"We'll see," Sonya said.

It amused John-Michael to see Sonya playing the patient parent figure, Muffy the petulant child. He and his father had experienced that reversal many years ago, but he'd never expected to see it between these two. In his mind, Sonya was the eternal child, the spoiled princess, and Muffy the overindulgent but firm mama.

Sonya had seemed different, though, since her trip. More mature, more serious, more assertive. Unfortunately for his mental well-being, more attractive, too. He would have to adjust his thinking.

"I'll leave you two alone," he said, moving toward the door.

"Oh, John-Mikey," Muffy said, using his childhood nickname. Muffy was the only person who could get away with that. Not even Jock tried it. "Could you bring me something to eat? Maybe a nice blueberry muffin?" She batted her eyelashes. "The breakfast they served me was pitiful."

"Don't you dare," Sonya said. "She's not getting one bite of anything the doctor didn't prescribe. But I understand if you'd like to get something for yourself," she added. "I did get you up rather early this morning and didn't even offer you breakfast."

"I think I will get something," he said gruffly. "I'll see you in a few minutes." John-Michael slipped out the door, needing some space and distance from Sonya. He wasn't sure he liked her being polite to him, nice, even. Such behavior upset the world order. It was much better that he treat her like a contemptible snail.

She'd started to be a little bit nice last night, too, sharing her macaroni and cheese. And he'd felt that familiar pull. She'd looked so approachable, all rumpled in her night clothes, her silky robe and nightgown showing far too much of her body's contours to be considered modest.

That was why he'd deliberately picked a fight with her, calling her spoiled. Nothing was as certain to get her dander up. And he needed her mad at him. When she was nice, she was too damn tempting. And this added dimension she'd recently acquired, this mysterious allure he'd never noticed before, only added to the overall package.

SONYA HAD THOUGHT that, once she and her mother were alone, she might broach the subject of calling off the wedding altogether. Though she wasn't ready to admit she'd been seduced, conned, dumped and picked clean, she couldn't allow the wedding plans to continue. Her mother had already spent a fortune on the preparations, much of it nonrefundable.

But Muffy's first words, once they were alone, changed her plans. She grasped Sonya's hand with more strength than a woman so recently at death's door should have been able to muster. "Sonya, promise me something."

"I'll try. But I won't smuggle you any of Thomas's cheesecake." Thomas was Muffy's favorite dessert chef, from the Cheesecake Emporium.

"No, be serious. You can't postpone the wedding."

"Mother—"

"Listen to me. Planning that wedding was…the most fun I've ever had in my life, more fun than planning…my own, even."

"I know," Sonya said. "But the stress—"

"Oh, stress, schmess. I was enjoying myself, and having fun never caused a heart attack."

Sonya knew differently. Even good stress could affect the body in negative ways.

"Years of ignoring my doctor's advice—and yours—are what made me sick," Muffy continued. "But as I was lying on that gurney in the emergency room, and I heard them yell 'Code Blue!', only one thing kept me alive. I kept telling myself, 'you have to get through this for Sonya's wedding. You can't miss Sonya's wedding.'"

"Oh, Mother…"

"We can't delay it. What if I have another heart attack and I don't make it?"

"That's not going to happen. Your doctor told me—"

"Doctors don't know everything. We can't predict the future. Promise me…" She paused to catch her breath. "Promise me you'll carry on with the preparations, that we'll do it on January 8, just as planned."

Her heart dropped like a rock thrown down a well. The last thing she needed was to continue the pretense that she was going to marry that skunk. "Of course, Mother." What else could she say? She'd straighten everything out when her mother's health was better, when she was in no danger of relapsing. Meanwhile, she would have to pretend she was still a blushing bride-to-be.

THREE DAYS LATER Muffy's health had dramatically improved. She was walking, talking in a normal voice, eating normally—if hospital food could be called normal for Muffy, which it couldn't—and begging to be let out of the hospital. She chose to sit in her chair rather than in bed, looking resplendent in the quilted silk bed jacket her friend Tootsie had given her. She'd brought her manicurist in for a fresh set of tips and her hairstylist to reshape the flattened poof of her red-gold hair. She was even wearing makeup.

Per Muffy's request, Sonya had brought her Daytimer and her Rolodex, and was now making a long list of tasks that had to be attended to ASAP for the wedding. Her cardiologist happened to visit during this heated planning session, and Sonya was positive he was going to put the kybosh on it. She was, in fact, hoping Dr. Cason would tell Muffy that she was not to even *think* about something as stressful as her daughter's wedding for at least six months.

Unfortunately, the exact opposite happened. Dr. Cason took one look at Muffy, noting the sparkle in her eye and the roses in her cheeks and the smiles and laughter, and he declared planning a wedding to be the secret, curative tonic everyone was looking for.

"But, Dr. Cason," Sonya ventured, "don't you think this wedding is too stressful for her right now? I've told her we could postpone it."

"No," Muffy said, "absolutely not. That would mean starting all over, rebooking the orchestra and the country club, and who knows if our first choices will be available? It would be horrible, much more stressful than merely putting the finishing touches on what we've already planned."

Dr. Cason grinned. "I think your mother's right, Sonya. Look at her. She's smiling and laughing, and studies have shown a happy attitude to be one of the key factors in recovering from cardiac illness."

"And I won't overdo, I promise," Muffy wheedled. "Sonya can do all the running around and dealing with people. I'll just recline on my chaise lounge, eating my steamed broccoli and drinking skimmed milk—" she shuddered slightly "—and directing her efforts."

"Sounds like a plan," Cason said, no help at all.

Of course, McPhee was listening to the whole exchange. She looked to him for help, but he remained silent. It was only after they were once again in the back seat of the limo that he voiced his opinion.

"You seem awfully anxious to postpone the wedding."

"Nonsense. I can't wait to marry Marvin. But of course I want to do what's best for Mother."

"Have you talked to Marvin yet?"

"Yes. Yes, he called last night. He was horrified to hear about Mother and he's going to come home as soon as he can."

Then McPhee did something odd. He closed the glass partition between them and Tim. Normally everybody talked freely in front of Tim, who was the soul of discretion. He'd been driving for the Pattersons since before Sonya was born.

"I'm sure Marvin's parents would be happy to know you've talked to him," McPhee said once they were hermetically sealed into the back seat. "Because they haven't seen or heard from him in three months." He dropped this bombshell casually, as if it were just normal conversation.

"Wh-what?" Sonya's heart hammered inside her chest so hard she thought it was trying to escape.

"I took a closer look at the report the security agency provided on Marvin Carter III. He really is the oldest son in a very wealthy Boston family. Has quite a pedigree."

"Well, of course he is!" Sonya said somewhat desperately. She could tell by the sound of McPhee's voice that he had something up his sleeve. And he was about to drop it on her.

"He's also a habitual thief. The family has done a good job of hiding it from the public. Arrest records purged, charges dropped, people paid off. But about three months ago he disappeared. Family has no idea where he is, and frankly they're hoping he won't turn up. I did a bit more digging and discovered he's wanted by the FBI in connection with some art and jewelry thefts."

"Where did you hear such nonsense?" But her trembling voice gave her away. He knew. He knew everything.

"How much did he take from you, Sonya?"

"I don't know what you're talking about."

"I notice you don't wear much jewelry anymore, other than your engagement ring."

She nervously twisted the two-carat, pear-shaped solitaire that sat on her left ring finger. She'd had it checked. It was a very convincing cubic zirconia. She looked out the tinted window. Then she rummaged in her purse until she found a lipstick and reapplied the color and powdered her nose.

"This isn't going to go away," McPhee said. "The longer you stay in denial, the worse it will be when the truth comes out. And it will, believe me. Sooner or later the press will get wind of it."

Sonya put her face in her hands. Why did McPhee, of all people, have to find out? Wouldn't he have just a grand time, rubbing her nose in her stupidity, rubbing salt in her wounds? He'd told her from the beginning he thought something wasn't right about Marvin.

"Your new friends, Brenna and Cindy. They were Marvin's victims, too?"

Sonya nodded, her face still hidden. She couldn't bear to look at McPhee, to see that knowing smirk that was surely on his face.

McPhee lowered the glass and said something to Tim, though she couldn't hear what. The blood was pounding too loudly in her ears. A few minutes later the limo parked.

"Be right back," McPhee said.

Sonya looked up then. They were in a strip shopping center. She had no idea what McPhee was up to and she didn't care. She just wanted to take advantage of his absence and pull herself together. McPhee was right, she couldn't play the denial game anymore. Now she had to draw on all her strength and make some decisions. If she crumbled, others would make decisions for her, as they'd done most of her life, and she wasn't going to let that happen. Now now. Not when the stakes were so high.

With the decision made to own up to the true situation, Sonya felt better, stronger. She reminded herself that her friends Brenna and Cindy had benefited after taking a strong stand against Marvin. Cindy had recovered her restaurant and at least some of her money, and Brenna had tracked down the Picasso painting Marvin had stolen from her parents, as well as some of her jewelry. It was time for Sonya to pull her head out of the sand and resume the fight.

When McPhee returned to the limo a few minutes later, Sonya was sitting upright, posture erect, hands folded demurely in her lap, her face a mask of haughty detachment. She'd learned that face from Muffy. It was the one she wore in the fact of any disaster. "Never let anyone see you crying," Muffy had told a ten-year-old Sonya after her father's funeral, when she'd inquired why her mother had remained dry-eyed and stern-faced during the service. "If you must cry at all, tears are for when you're alone."

Then she realized McPhee was holding out a grande toffee-nut latte from Starbucks—one of her many weaknesses. "I had them make it with whole milk instead of skim, and extra whipped cream," he said. "You don't look like you need to lose any more weight."

The small kindness almost undid her. She wasn't used to McPhee being kind or sympathetic, not in recent history. Courteous, yes. Always mindful of her needs, always quick to do her bidding. As she took the coffee drink, she glanced over at him. No sign of a smirk. He looked genuinely worried.

"I told Tim to just drive around for a while," he said. "I want to hear the whole story. I need to know what happened if I'm going to help you keep this thing contained. Now, let's start from the beginning. How much did he take from you?"

Resigned, she told him what he wanted to know. "Not as much as he took from some of his other victims. I didn't have a lot of easily accessible cash, just what was in my checking account—about thirty-five thousand dollars. He couldn't get at my trust fund, which I'm sure was what he was hoping for. But he did take all my jewelry, which was worth a considerable sum." She'd collected quite a few baubles over the years. Her mother was fond of giving her jewelry for just about any occasion—the larger and more unusual, the better.

Sonya took another sip of the rich, sweet coffee drink. The warmth was welcome, since she was shivering.

"He took three fur coats," she continued. "A sable, a mink and a fox." Not that she ever wore them. They were gifts, too, and very impractical, given that it seldom got cold enough for fur in Houston. Besides, fur coats were very un-PC.

"So Marvin was engaged to Brenna *and* Cindy *and* you at the same time?"

"Yes. Cindy had a lot of cash from her first husband's life insurance. Her parents had left her money and property, too, as well as a restaurant, so I'm sure she was quite attractive to Marvin. Brenna is the heiress to a chi-chi department store in Dallas."

"How did you locate them?"

"I found Brenna's phone number in the call history of Marvin's cell phone."

McPhee arched one eyebrow. "And why were you looking there?"

"I'd started to suspect he had a girlfriend," she admitted. "All those long absences when he was supposedly traveling on business. Whispered phone calls at odd times. So I snooped. But I didn't try to contact her until after Marvin left with all my stuff. When I was supposed to be at the spa, I went to see Brenna instead. She had a lead on a third victim, who turned out to be Cindy. She lives in Cottonwood—that's why we went there. By the time we found her, she'd already lost everything.

"Holy cow. Were there more victims?"

"He was working on a bank teller in Louisiana. Her father owned the bank. He was planning some sort of scam to get access to the bank's computer system. But we caught up with him before he could actually steal anything from her. Flushed him out. We recovered some of Cindy's money, but Marvin got away." She laughed. "He had to run naked down Main Street to get away from us."

She chanced another look at McPhee and realized she'd surprised him. He was staring at her, slack-jawed. "Let me get this straight," he said when he'd recovered from the shock. "You went with Brenna and Cindy— those two pretty blondes I met a couple of weeks ago when you went to Dallas—on a manhunt? That's what you were doing all that time you were out of town? That's why you were in New Orleans?"

"Yes. Then there was New York."

"You went to New York?" McPhee asked in a voice that sounded fearful of her answer.

"No, silly. But Brenna did. She and Agent Packer had him cornered at that jewelry show."

"The one you were helping her get ready for?"

Sonya nodded. "Marvin escaped by jumping down an elevator shaft." The story had been reported on *CNN*, and even the *Houston Chronicle* had run a piece on it. Thankfully, Marvin's real name hadn't been mentioned in either story.

"It's all starting to fit together now," McPhee said thoughtfully. "But it's weird. I never thought of you as one of Charlie's Angels."

"As I've pointed out before," she said with exaggerated patience, "you don't know everything about me. What's more, I intend to continue the hunt for Marvin. He's getting bolder and greedier. Pretty soon he's bound to do something really stupid and get himself caught. Or get somebody hurt."

"It's too dangerous. You can't—"

"I can, and I will. Mother's illness derailed my participation, but once we get her squared away, I'm back in it. Law enforcement isn't making much of an effort. Marvin didn't murder anyone or rob a bank, so he's a low priority."

"What about Packer?"

"He was the only FBI agent to take the case seriously, but then he got fired, and when he recovered the stolen Picasso they tried to give him his job back, but he refused, and now he's a private investigator."

McPhee squeezed the bridge of his nose between thumb and forefinger, as if he had a headache. "Stolen Picasso?"

Sonya was pleased to have surprised McPhee. As she recalled how strong she and the other women—"The Blondes," as the people of Cottonwood had dubbed them—had been together, she felt a surge of power wash through her. The feelings of helplessness and inadequacy that she'd almost succumbed to a few minutes earlier receded. She wasn't just a spoiled debutante, no matter what McPhee thought. She was smart and capable, and she could accomplish great things when she put her mind to it.

"We think Marvin might have gone to—"

McPhee held up a hand to halt her explanations. "Please, I can't take any more of this. You've thrown my whole universe off balance."

"Good," she said with a smile. "You need that, sometimes."

JOHN-MICHAEL LEANED BACK against the limo's buttery leather seat, stunned to the core. He'd known Sonya was harboring a secret. He'd tried to put it together a couple of weeks ago, when she'd taken a quick weekend trip to Dallas to help Brenna prepare for a jewelry show. He'd discovered then that she had another new friend, Cindy, from Cottonwood, Texas, and the three of them had behaved the way closely bonded, longtime friends act. He knew there was a story there, but he'd been at a loss. He hadn't gotten many facts out of Heath Packer, either. The FBI agent had been friendly to John-Michael, and his personal interest in Brenna had been apparent, but he'd volunteered little information as to the nature of the friendship among the three women. By the time John-Michael and Sonya had returned to Houston, he'd been no wiser.

His theory had been that Sonya had a lover. That would have been shocking enough. But to find out she'd been living a clandestine life hunting down a criminal blew him away. He could hardly wrap his mind around it.

Sonya, pensive now after her long, convoluted explanation, took another sip of her latte, leaving a slight whipped-cream mustache. She licked it off.

Not now, John-Michael thought disgustedly. Now

was not the time for his sporadic lust for Sonya Patterson to rear its ugly head. He'd been dealing with it for years, and usually all it took was a sharp reminder of exactly who Sonya was—a spoiled, useless little rich girl with nothing more important on her mind than her next manicure appointment—to cool his desire. Physically she might be a pure turn-on, but he'd long ago learned to look beyond a woman's body to the substance of her. Pretty girls were a dime a dozen, and he had no trouble attracting them. But finding one who was pretty *and* intelligent *and* interesting—that's what it took to capture John-Michael's libido for more than thirty seconds.

Sonya had become suddenly interesting, damn it. Perhaps she had a lot more behind that cool demeanor than she let on. She did have a degree in chemical engineering from Rice University, and graduating from that school was no cakewalk. But frankly, he'd assumed Sonya's family wealth had bought the degree. Her mother had donated buckets of money to her father's alma mater. And he'd never seen Sonya study much while she was in college.

This was a helluva time for him to start thinking of her as more than arm candy. He had a future planned, a life apart from the Pattersons. He'd actually been looking forward to moving on. Now, suddenly, he wasn't so sure.

He forced himself to think about freezing cold waterfalls and cornmeal mush until his jeans were no longer quite so tight. Then he returned to the matter at hand.

"When are you going to tell Muffy?"

Her eyes widened in alarm. "I'm not. Are you kidding? The news would kill her! Dr. Cason said we had to keep her smiling and laughing."

"You'll have to tell her at some point. I mean, let's face it, the groom isn't going to show up for this wedding."

Sonya started to chew on one of her nails, then quickly stopped herself. She used to bite her nails as a child, he remembered. It was only when she'd discovered acrylic-sculptured nails that she'd been able to stop.

"I'll tell her when she's stronger," Sonya said. "But not now, not yet. She's not even out of the hospital. And you can't tell her, either," she said, suddenly fierce. "You can't tell anyone. *No one* is to know that this wedding isn't going to take place."

"Don't you think people are going to get a little suspicious when they never see the groom-to-be? Isn't his absence going to be noted?"

"I've already told people he travels on business a lot. And he supposedly lives in Boston. Anyway, most men are weddingphobic. They won't come near the preparations. No one will think it's odd in the least, believe me."

"But…you can't just let your mother keep throwing money at a wedding that won't ever happen," John-Michael objected. "Doesn't it strike you as a bit cruel to lie to her, to keep up the pretense? The farther along you get with this thing, the harder it's going to be when you have to call it off."

Damned right it would be hard. And he wasn't helping. But Muffy could stand to throw away a few bucks
a lot more easily than her heart could stand an emotional
shock. And somehow Sonya would figure out a way to
pay her back. "As soon as her doctor says she's well
enough to handle gruesomely unpleasant news, I'll tell
her. But not before. McPhee, promise me. Not a word."

"All right, I promise." What choice did he have? He
wasn't going to be responsible for causing Muffy a second heart attack. But his instincts warned him that the
longer they maintained the lie, the messier it was going
to get, for all parties concerned.

Chapter Three

It was December, almost a month after Muffy's heart attack, that she finally came home. Then the real fun began.

Sonya, still feeling guilty for having been away from home and out of touch when Muffy was stricken ill, appointed herself sole guardian of Muffy's health. That meant learning all of the doctor's instructions and seeing that they were followed to the letter.

It also meant limiting her mother's social calendar. Dr. Cason had emphasized that social visits, while pleasant, were tiring. Some activity was desirable, but getting enough rest, so the heart could heal, was essential.

Tootsie proved to be Sonya's first big challenge. She showed up less than an hour after Muffy's homecoming.

"She has to rest," Sonya said, standing squarely in the front doorway, refusing to even allow Tootsie in the house. Tootsie had come to the hospital almost every day, staying hour after hour, gossiping endlessly until the nurses threw her out. Once she got inside the house, there would be no getting rid of her. "And you may *not* give her those chocolates. Tootsie, what's the matter with you? She's had a heart attack! She's on a restricted diet."

Tootsie rolled her eyes. "There will be plenty of time for all that dreary cardiac rehab stuff when Muffy's feeling better," said Tootsie, herself thin and straight as a fencepost. She'd likely never had to worry about extra pounds and the resulting health concerns. "I went through this with my husband. Now don't be a brat." She smiled insincerely. "I won't stay long."

Tootsie's husband had died after his third heart attack. It was tacky to hold Tootsie responsible, but she certainly couldn't be held up as an expert in cardiac aftercare.

Sonya threw her arm across the doorway. "I'm sorry, Tootsie, but I'm going to have to insist…" Her words trailed off as she realized Tootsie wasn't listening. She was looking over Sonya's shoulder and smiling like a cunning cat with a canary on its mind.

Sonya knew who was behind her without looking. Tootsie had always enjoyed ogling John-Michael, not that Sonya could blame her for that.

"Why, John-Michael," Tootsie purred, "aren't you looking…fine today. Would you tell your little charge here to let me inside? Muffy will think her best friend has abandoned her if I don't visit her every single day."

Sonya gritted her teeth at being referred to as McPhee's "little charge."

McPhee put his hand around Sonya's arm and gently moved it, allowing Tootsie inside. "Mrs. Patterson is with her physical therapist right now, and she asked that she not be disturbed. If you'd care to wait, she'll be done in a couple of hours."

Tootsie consulted her diamond Piaget watch. "Oh, I can't wait. I have an appointment to get the Caddy serviced. I'll come back later. Would you see that Muffy gets these?" She handed the box of chocolates to McPhee.

"Of course."

Tootsie turned and headed right back out the door, then paused on the porch to look over her shoulder at Sonya. "Pretty big for your britches, now that you're getting married to a millionaire, huh?"

Sonya took a step back. She was used to Tootsie's veiled putdowns, but not overt antagonism.

"Just remember, I knew Muffy for twenty years before you were born. I know what she needs most, and she doesn't need to be treated like some invalid."

Astonished, Sonya watched Tootsie climb into her Cadillac. That woman had some nerve. And speaking of nerve… As the Caddy roared off, Sonya turned to see John Michael opening the box of chocolates Tootsie had shoved at him.

"You aren't giving those to Mother."

"Of course not. Want one?"

"No, I don't want one! I can't believe you just overruled me like that! You moved my arm like it was nothing and let her in."

"I got rid of her, didn't I?"

Come to think of it, he had.

"I was using psychology on her," he explained. "You have to make Tootsie believe she's the one making the decisions. She hates waiting around, so I knew she wouldn't when I gave her the option."

"The physical therapist isn't really here, is she?"

"She's scheduled for two o'clock. Are you sure you don't want a chocolate?"

"You know I do. Why do you even tempt me?" Sonya had a wicked sweet tooth, but she usually didn't let herself have candy. She had a tendency not to stop once she started.

He popped a chocolate-covered caramel into his mouth. Speaking of temptations, she wished he wouldn't parade around the house in gym shorts and a snug T-shirt that showed off every muscle. Didn't he know it was December? No wonder Tootsie had practically drooled.

He held the box out to her. "You don't exactly need to worry about gaining weight."

Sonya *had* dropped some weight. And chocolate was an antioxidant and an antidepressant, she rationalized. Sonya remembered reading that happy news in the books on diet and nutrition Dr. Cason had given her. She reconsidered the chocolate. "Maybe I'll have just one piece—for the therapeutic value, of course."

"Of course." He extended the box toward her.

After making a careful inspection of the available candies, she selected one that looked like it had almonds in it. "Almonds are just bursting with Omega-3 fatty acids," she said, and settled it gently on her tongue. The candy was exquisite. Of course, Tootsie never bought anything that wasn't first-rate and superexpensive. Sonya chose another, a miniature cherry truffle. Cherries were fruits. That had to be healthy. "Oh, my, these are good."

McPhee set the box down on a small gilt table in the foyer, which was flanked by two delicate Louis XV chairs. He sat in one, and Sonya automatically sat in the other. No way was she going to let him hog all that chocolate.

"We really should share these," she said.

"The box has three layers. Plenty for all."

"Oh, okay." Sonya picked out a toffee. "I wish I knew how you manipulated Tootsie so easily. If *I* had told her she couldn't visit Mother during physical therapy, she'd have just argued me into the ground until she got her way."

"She's old-fashioned. She defers to males, even if they're only servants."

"I don't think of you as a 'servant,'" she said, feeling charitable. Chocolate had that effect on her. "You're part of the family." She realized how stupid that sounded almost before the words had left her lips.

McPhee laughed, soft and deep in his throat. The sound vibrated along Sonya's nerve endings. "Funny, I don't feel at all like a brother."

Sonya stuffed another chocolate into her mouth. She didn't even make a careful selection this time, just grabbed the one closest. He was right, of course. She never would have treated a brother as coldly as she'd treated McPhee over the past ten years. But she never would have had romantic feelings for a brother, either.

Once she'd let the lid off that particular Pandora's Box, there'd been no going back. It would have been one thing if he'd returned her feelings. But when he'd indicated with crystal clarity that he was not open to romance, her only other choice had been coldness. To get over him, she'd had to convince herself she hated him.

She didn't, of course. Never had. And she'd never exactly gotten over him. Even when Marvin had come along and swept her off her feet, she'd still sometimes lain awake at night, wondering how it might have been if McPhee had responded to her romantic overtures that night so long ago.

Now, maybe it was time she got over it. She wasn't some teenager with a crush, even if she still felt that way sometimes. She was grown up. Holding on to a ten-year-old grudge was stupid, especially when she knew McPhee couldn't help it that he hadn't wanted to get involved with her. Just as she hadn't been able to control her own emotions.

"McPhee, I've been horrible to you. And I'd like to apologize. I know one apology can't make up for ten years of bitchiness…"

"Whoa, whoa!" McPhee shook his head, as if trying to clear his mind of some untenable thought. "Did you just apologize to me?"

"I was trying to. But if you're going to be ugly about it—"

"No, please. Go on."

She tried to ignore the trace of amusement evident in the set of his mouth, the sparkle in his brown eyes. "Mother's illness has brought some things into focus for me. You just never know when you're going to lose someone. I want to appreciate the people in my life before they're gone and it's too late."

"I…thanks. Does this mean you forgive me?"

"For what?" she asked, pretending she didn't know what he was talking about.

"You know what. That night. When everything changed."

"Oh, that." She waved away the notion that it was important. "I had too much to drink and I put you in an awkward position."

"I could have handled the situation with a little more tact."

"It's ancient history, as far as I'm concerned." And she was very proud of herself for having such a mature discussion about it. "We should have cleared the air about that years ago. But better now than never. I don't want us to be enemies," she added.

"No, I don't want that, either. I don't want to leave here on bad terms with you."

Sonya sat up straighter. Suddenly all that burgeoning maturity fled like a flock of sparrows when a hungry cat jumps into their midst. 'You're not really leaving, are you?"

He looked at her the way he used to when she would ask a particularly dumb question about motorcycle maintenance. "I already told you that, right? That I'm going to work for the Sheriff's Department?"

"Yes, but that was when you thought I was getting married."

"I'm still going. My last day is still January 8."

"But Mother—"

"—will have to get used to the idea. I want to go now, while my father is determined to stay off the sauce. If I stay, it might give him an excuse to give up, since he knows I'll be here to rescue him."

A few days ago, Sonya had actually been worried that she'd be stuck with her bodyguard for the rest of her life. She should have been immensely relieved that she would finally be rid of him.

But what she felt wasn't relief, she was pretty sure.

She reached for another chocolate, but McPhee slid the box out of her reach. "You're going to be sick if you eat any more of those."

Come to think of it, she did feel uncomfortably full. How many had she eaten? Three? Four?

"You ate seven," McPhee said, reading her mind in that annoying way he had.

"Seven! Oh, why did you even let me get started? You know how I am."

"You're not exactly the queen of moderation," he agreed.

"How many did you eat?" She started to count the empty squares, hoping to discover he'd eaten at least as many as she, but he put the lid on the box.

"I'll get rid of the rest."

"Good idea."

"So I'm forgiven?" he persisted.

"Assuming you don't force me to eat any more of those chocolates. Or do anything between now and January 8 to make me mad."

"Sometimes all I have to do is say 'Good morning' to make you mad."

She stood and gave him an imperious look, but for some reason she was about to laugh and ruin her exit line. "You'll want to try not to smirk at me when you say 'Good morning.'"

"I do not smirk."

"You do. In a really annoying and condescending way like one of those English servants who know everything. Admit it."

"It's possible," he said carefully, "that I sometimes lift a sardonic eyebrow in a sort of Heathcliff-esque way. I wouldn't refer to it as a smirk, which would involve pursing my mouth in some unattractive manner."

"You're getting into semantics now. Whatever you call it, a smirk or a sardonic eyebrow lift, it gets my goat. If you'll make an effort to stop doing it, I will try not to get mad more often than you really deserve." And she whisked out of the room in search of some Pepcid.

JOHN-MICHAEL WATCHED HER GO, his stomach lurching in an odd way that had nothing to do with eating too many chocolates. Who was this woman? She certainly wasn't acting like the spoiled debutante. She'd jumped out of that neat pigeonhole into which he'd had her safely stuffed all these years. And he wasn't comfortable with the situation, not at all.

A spoiled, petulant Sonya, putting him in his place, was far easier to deal with than a kind, sensitive, funny Sonya. She'd actually shown him her sense of humor just now, something she hadn't directed his way in forever. First he'd had to accept her cloak-and-dagger activities. Now this.

All right, he was going to have to face the fact. His lust for Sonya was turning into something else, something dangerous. For the first time in many years, he wasn't sure he could hold himself back, pretend indifference.

But maybe he didn't have to. Hell, he was soon to be off the Patterson payroll. Sonya would no longer be forbidden fruit. He let himself roll that idea around in his head, intrigued with it.

Whistling, he carried the chocolates into the kitchen, where he found Matilda. Normally the roly-poly Patterson cook was perky as one of her own orange-marmalade muffins. But ever since Muffy's heart attack, Matilda had been sulking over the fact that she had to completely change the way she prepared Muffy's meals. Now he found her sifting through her recipe box, sorting cards into "keep" and "throw away" piles. The throw-away pile was much larger than the keeper.

She eyed the box of chocolates suspiciously. "Oh, so it's all right for you to be peddling this fattening stuff," she said as she took two candies, "but not me?"

"You don't have any heart problems, do you?"

"Not a one. Doc says I'm healthy as a horse. Good genes."

"Well, not all of us were born so lucky. C'mon, Mattie, you can adapt. Think of it as a challenge, a chance to try some new recipes."

"But those recipes Mrs. Patterson's doctor gave me are so boring, so tasteless."

"So, invent your own recipes. Maybe if you and Eric work together you can come up with some gourmet heart-healthy recipes and we can all eat healthier."

"Healthier, right." She nodded toward the candy. "Where did you get those?"

"Tootsie. Sensitive soul that she is, she brought them for Mrs. Patterson."

"Ugh! What's she trying to do, kill her best friend? Just because she's a skinny twig and can eat anything she wants. Take those chocolates out of here."

"Mattie?" said a disembodied voice. "Mattie, are you there?" It was Muffy on the intercom.

Matilda walked over to the kitchen unit, on the wall near the phone. "Yes, Mrs. Patterson?"

"Could you send my daughter up here? I can't find her."

"She's probably hiding from you," Matilda said without pushing the talk button, and John-Michael smiled. Muffy was loving all the attention having a heart attack brought her. She'd always been something of a hypochondriac, imagining that every ache and pain was the symptom of a fatal tumor. Now that she had an actual illness, she took full advantage of having everyone at her beck and call, especially Sonya. She'd become quite the tyrant.

Unfortunately, Sonya was feeling the strain. She had a hard time saying no to Muffy, so long as what Muffy wanted didn't jeopardize her recovery.

John-Michael pushed the intercom button. "Is it anything I can help you with, Mrs. Patterson?"

"No, it's wedding stuff. I've just located the most wonderful Belgian lace for Sonya's gown. It's in Los Angeles, of all places. She'll have to go there personally to pick out the pattern she wants, though I have some ideas. And I'll want you to go, too, of course."

A trip to California didn't sound so bad, he mused. A warm beach, Sonya in a bikini… "I'll find her."

He searched all over the estate until he finally located Sonya swimming laps in the indoor pool. When she was stressed he could usually find her here or working out on the treadmill or soaking in the whirlpool.

He waited at one end of the pool until she completed a series of laps. When she paused to catch her breath, he called her name.

"Huh?" she sputtered. "Oh."

"Working off some stress?"

"Working off some calories. Of course, it would take about a million laps to burn off all that candy." She hoisted herself out of the pool, and he handed her her towel. She wasn't wearing a bikini, but an ultra-modest tank suit.

"Your mom wants to talk to you."

Sonya sighed. "Okay. Is it urgent? I was planning to sit in the sauna."

"Something about Belgian lace in California. She wants you to go there personally and pick it out."

"I am *not* going to California." She blotted herself with the towel and suddenly the coverage wasn't enough. Sure there was fabric over all the key areas, but the way it clung…

John-Michael suddenly couldn't figure out where to direct his gaze. He couldn't look at her when her nipples showed plainly through her pale-green suit. But if he looked away, she would know he was deliberately *not* looking at her.

"It was bad enough when I spent two days in Dallas," she continued, oblivious to his discomfort. "But Mother was in the hospital under constant medical supervision. Now I'm the one responsible for her care. I can't leave."

"There are plenty of people here to look after Muffy. Anyway, she's not an invalid."

"But her medications—"

"She can handle them. Her heart suffered a blow, but her brain is fine. Sonya, you need a break. You've hardly left your mother's side for an entire month. She loves the attention, but she needs to start taking responsibility for her own care. It's a good sign that she's willing to turn you loose for a couple of days. You should take advantage of it."

"Yeah, but all the way to California? To pick out lace for a dress I'm not going to wear?"

"Can you think of a nicer place to go in December?" he countered.

"We could look for Marvin! Maybe we could visit his parents in Boston and see if they could help us."

That was one idea John-Michael didn't want to encourage. The idea of Sonya chasing after some felon with no thought of the danger made his teeth hurt. But now that she'd landed on the idea, she seemed enamored with it. "I'll call Cindy and Brenna. This'll be fun."

"Fun?"

"Fun," she confirmed. "It was terrible, what Marvin did to us, what he might be doing to another woman even as we speak. But when I tracked down Brenna, and then together we found Cindy, and then the three of us were working together to catch Marvin—it was the most fun I've ever had in my life."

The way her eyes sparkled just recalling her adventure, John-Michael didn't doubt her words. She was more animated than he could remember seeing her. And he was turned on more than he wanted to admit. Thankfully, she wasn't paying attention to him or she might have noticed. His gym shorts didn't hide much.

"You really like those girls, huh?"

"I feel that for the first time in my life I have friends, real friends."

"You've always had a lot of friends."

"I've always had lots of girls around me," she corrected him. "But the rich girls flocked together because of our parents' money and the insular world we lived in, not because we necessarily were drawn together by common interests. And a lot of girls made friends with me because of what they thought I could do for them. They wanted to hang out here, have Matilda cook for them and wait on them, have Muffy take us all out to lunch at the ritziest restaurants.

"But Brenna and Cindy—I know they like me for me. Neither one of them cares about being rich or having the latest designer whatever or seeing their names mentioned in a magazine. And the more time I spent with them, the more I started to realize where my priorities ought to be."

Sonya toweled her hair dry, and it formed a tousled blond cloud around her head. Left to its own devices, it tended to curl wildly. He liked it better this way, John-Michael decided. Sort of like she'd just tumbled out of bed.

He clamped down on that line of thought. He'd long ago learned not to wish for something he couldn't have. Oh, maybe he could have had Sonya once upon a time. In the back seat of his car, or sneaking into spare bedrooms when Muffy was away. But that would never have satisfied him. He didn't want to be a rich girl's walk on the wild side.

Anything more was out of the question. Debutantes did not marry their bodyguards.

Of course, he wasn't going to be just a bodyguard forever. He had a future now. He had a career beyond the World of Patterson. He would be someone independent of this family and their wealth. Someone who could be taken seriously…

"McPhee?"

The sound of his name brought him back.

"You zoned out there for a second. Sorry. I must have bored you silly with all that talk about friendship and adventure and having a purpose to my life. Those are probably lessons you learned a long time ago."

"You didn't bore me," he said. What she'd done was set his own imagination into overdrive. But now he forced himself back to reality. Yeah, he was looking forward to starting his job in law enforcement. But he'd still never be able to even take Sonya out for dinner. He was still the gardener's son.

Chapter Four

Sonya felt better than she had in days. She'd gotten up before dawn and packed. Now she was eating shredded wheat, fruit and skim milk—part of Matilda's new menus—and looking forward to a trip to Cottonwood. Brenna was meeting her there, and they were all going to stay at the B&B. Luke, Cindy's husband, was off for the weekend, and he'd agreed to look after Adam, Cindy's toddler.

Yesterday she'd spoken to the nice woman in Los Angeles who imported the Belgian lace and explained that she wouldn't be visiting after all. Then, out of guilt, she'd ordered ten yards of the stuff sight unseen. If it didn't arrive at some point, Muffy would wonder.

McPhee wandered into the kitchen just as Sonya added a few more blueberries to her bowl, then some toasted, slivered almonds for good measure. Anything to give the cereal some flavor.

"Is that breakfast?" he asked, nodding toward the box of shredded wheat. McPhee didn't need any extra flavor. He looked delicious in a pair of khakis and a starched burgundy shirt. He'd even gotten a haircut, though Sonya didn't mind it when he grew his hair out longer. "What happened to waffles and bacon?"

"You won't find them here."

"Just because Muffy's on a restricted diet, do the rest of us have to endure it?" he grumbled, getting himself a bowl and spoon from the cabinet.

"We could all stand to eat better," Sonya said. "So in thirty years we won't be in cardiac rehab. Are you packed?"

"Yeah. Are we taking the limo?"

"The last time we took the limo through Cottonwood, we nearly caused a riot." Cindy had gotten a kick out of it, but Sonya didn't want to draw that kind of attention when she was trying to keep a low profile. "My car will be less obtrusive."

"I'm driving," McPhee said.

"Says who?"

"Says anyone who's seen you drive." He watched, waiting for her to take the bait and escalate the argument.

But she was in too good a mood to argue. Besides, he was right. She hardly ever drove her own car, so she wasn't confident behind the wheel. Either Tim chauffeured her in the limo, or she let John-Michael drive. He'd been trained, after all, in evasive maneuvers in case there was ever a kidnapping attempt.

"All right, you can drive," she said. "But I'll never get better if I don't practice."

"You're certainly easy to get along with this morning."

She shrugged. It was true. The prospect of working with Brenna and Cindy again, as a team, filled her with joy. When they were tracking Marvin, she'd had a role, a purpose. And even if most of the time her most important function had been to bankroll the search with her credit card, she'd known her contribution was important.

"You have a very strange look on your face," McPhee said.

It was no wonder. She'd just had an epiphany. "McPhee, I never thought I'd be saying this, but you were right about me all along. I'm spoiled. And useless. I'm almost thirty years old and I don't do anything. I fill my days with social engagements and shopping."

"What about your charity work?"

"Oh, you mean those board meetings I attend once a month? Or the committees I serve on two or three times a year so I can maintain the illusion that my life has a purpose?"

"Maybe now is not the time to reevaluate your entire life," McPhee said, his voice gentle. "You're under a lot of stress, what with your mother's illness and the wedding and the little problem with Marvin—"

She groaned. "Marvin. What was I thinking? Even if he wasn't a conman, I was going to marry him and move to Boston and become another Muffy or, God forbid, a Tootsie."

"What alternative do you have?"

"I could…I don't know. Volunteer in a homeless shelter or a free clinic."

McPhee laughed, but the sharp look she gave him silenced him. Dear God, she was serious. And the look on her face right now was priceless. Sort of like a blond Scarlett O'Hara, declaring she would plant cotton. Except not as self-serving as Scarlett. Sonya might be spoiled, but she wasn't selfish.

"Or I could get a job."

"Doing what, exactly?" He didn't mean to ask it that way. But he simply could not picture Sonya Patterson with a job, getting up early every day, clocking in, eating lunch in a company cafeteria.

Fortunately she was so caught up in her fantasy that she hadn't noticed his slight derision. "Engineering, of course. I've always been interested in the development of alternate energy resources. Wind and solar. Even nuclear."

John-Michael slapped a hand over his mouth to prevent another burst of laughter.

"What?" she said sharply. "You don't think I'm smart enough?"

"No, no, of course you're smart enough. You have an engineering degree."

Sonya set her spoon in her empty bowl, pushed her chair back and slowly stood. "You don't think I could handle a job. You think I'd get bored or…or quit at the first sign of trouble."

That was exactly what he'd been thinking. But looking at her now, he had a sudden flash of insight. This woman was Muffy's daughter and she'd learned at least one lesson from her mother—to pick a goal and stick with it until she'd accomplished it. Sonya was determined. She would do what she set out to do.

She walked around the table and stood next to him. "Go ahead, McPhee, say it. You think I'm too lazy and pampered to work."

She was too close to him. He stood, intending to put some distance between them. Instead he took her in his arms and kissed her.

The initial contact of his mouth on hers was as much a shock to his system as it must have been to hers. She stiffened in surprise. But she didn't resist or make even a token attempt to pull away. As passions that had simmered for ten years flared to life so hot they could have burned a hole where they stood, Sonya's hands crept up to grip his arms, his shoulders, and finally the back of his neck.

The force of his kiss bent her head back. She groaned softly, the embrace shattering her rigid control as thoroughly as his hands devastated her carefully styled hair. He let the fingers of one hand creep under her sweater, brushing against the warm skin of her back. With his other hand, he cupped her small, firm bottom.

He and Sonya must have heard the squeak of Matilda's crepe-soled shoes on the marble tiles of the dining room floor at exactly the same time, because they sprang apart as if they'd been spring loaded. Sonya literally ran around to the other side of the table, grabbed her cereal bowl and lunged for the sink. She probably didn't realize that half of her hair had come loose from the pins and was hanging to her shoulders, or that her sweater was hiked up on one side.

All John-Michael could think to do was fall back into his chair just as Matilda entered the kitchen.

"Good morning to you, Sonya, and John-Michael. Don't you look nice. Your hair's shorter than usual."

"Got it cut yesterday," he mumbled, hastily wiping his mouth and chin with his napkin. A telltale smear of Sonya's raspberry-colored gloss was left on the napkin, making him wonder what Sonya's mouth looked like. But she was still facing the sink, scrubbing the cereal bowl to within an inch of its life.

What had happened? *What the hell had he just done?*

"Your mother is complaining bitterly about the shredded wheat," Matilda said as she put away the milk and cereal box. "Even the fresh blueberries and nuts aren't convincing her to like her healthy breakfast. She wants an omelet."

"Sh—she'll develop a taste for low-fat food," Sonya said, her voice coming out unnaturally squeaky.

Matilda glanced over at her, did a double take, apparently noticing the new, avant-garde hairstyle. But she didn't mention it. "Here, dear, let me take that. You don't have to scrub the dishes before you put them in the dishwasher, you know." She took the bowl from Sonya's hand and opened the dishwasher.

Sonya turned as she dried her hands on an embroidered tea towel. Her lip color was smeared everywhere. He urgently signaled her to wipe her mouth. After a moment of staring at him uncomprehendingly, she finally realized the problem and scrubbed at her face with a tea towel. By the time Matilda finished at the dishwasher, Sonya's face was flushed, her lips still full from being kissed. But there was nothing obviously indicating what had just happened, except the hair.

Sonya gave him a questioning look. *Better?*

He nodded, then surreptitiously pointed to his head. Sonya felt her hair and looked pained as she realized what it must look like.

"Oh, my gosh, I never finished putting up my hair," she said, laughing unconvincingly. "I guess I was so worried about missing our flight that I got into a big rush."

John-Michael saw a couple of hairpins on the floor. He leaned down and casually picked them up and stuck them in his shirt pocket.

"You'd better hurry and fix it," John-Michael said. "We should get going. No telling how the traffic will be."

"Oh, Sonya," Matilda said, "your mother wanted you to stop in and see her before you leave."

"Okay." Sonya scurried from the room, seeming eager for a chance to escape. He didn't blame her.

When she was gone, Matilda gave him a look. It was the sort of look she'd been giving him since he was old enough to filch cookies from her, and it made him want to confess every sin, great and small, he'd ever committed.

"I thought you were smarter than that."

Damn. He was so busted, he didn't bother with a denial. "Normally I am."

"I know she's a beautiful girl, John-Michael, but you've managed to keep your hands off for nearly thirty years."

"Only the last ten or so have been difficult."

"Don't be flippant, son," she said, and he could tell

she was deeply troubled by what she'd seen, or thought she knew. "That road brings nothing but heartache. I know you're leaving in a few weeks, and maybe that's made you reckless, but think of your father. Don't do anything that might reflect badly—"

"Matilda," he said to stop the torrent of motherly advice. Come to think of it, Matilda had been the closest thing to a mother he'd ever had. His own had died when he was three. "It was an isolated event. It won't happen again." At least not until he was officially off the Patterson payroll. Then all bets were off.

Sonya had kissed him back. She had *definitely* kissed him back. Which meant she might still feel something for him. It was definitely a starting place.

"See that it doesn't." She took his cereal bowl to the sink, though he wasn't finished with his breakfast.

"Matilda, I'm curious. How do you know I've kept my hands off all this time? How would you know if I hadn't?"

"I have instincts about these things, and I'm never wrong."

"Was she—is she sleeping with Marvin?"

"John-Michael McPhee, that is none of your business. And the fact that you're curious is a bad sign." She wet a sponge at the sink and began swabbing off the kitchen table. "Yes, she was sleeping with him, but only at his hotel. Never here."

"And when did she lose her virginity?"

"John-Michael!"

"I'm just testing your instincts against what I know."

"So you think you know?"

"I have my suspicions. I've spent more time with her than anyone else."

"It was on her class trip to Cancun. She was eighteen. You were at the police academy then, I believe."

"Hmm." He'd been wrong, then. He'd thought it was sometime later. That meant she'd not still been a virgin when she'd come on to him.

"It's inappropriate to be talking about this," Matilda said. "If Muffy knew you'd had even a single improper thought about her daughter, I don't know what she would do."

If Muffy didn't know that he thought Sonya was hot, she was blind to her daughter's allure and ignorant about the way men's minds worked. But Matilda was right—Muffy would go ballistic. She'd vetoed one boyfriend after another where Sonya was concerned, even the ones who came from wealthy families. Marvin was the only one who'd met with her full, unconditional approval.

This wasn't a good time for Muffy to go ballistic, John-Michael thought grimly. Which only strengthened his resolve to keep his libido in check—for now.

SONYA MADE A SIDE TRIP to a powder room before seeking out her mother, repairing her hair and makeup. Muffy would fuss if she ever saw Sonya looking less than well-groomed. Sonya couldn't imagine what she might think if she saw her daughter looking thoroughly ravished.

Hair fixed, nose powdered, lip gloss reapplied, she looked pretty good on the outside. Inside, she was still reeling. She'd fantasized at least a million times of just such a kiss, of John-Michael suddenly losing control and grabbing her. But she'd thought for a long time, now, that it was beyond impossible.

What had suddenly changed? Because he'd started it.

It wasn't her show of temper, because surely she'd shown him her temper many times. It wasn't her clothes. A pumpkin-colored cashmere sweater over fawn pants was hardly her sexiest outfit. Just yesterday he'd seen her in a swimsuit, and nothing had happened. Not to him, anyway. Her nipples had turned hard as glass beads just looking at him in his snug T-shirt, but she didn't think he'd even noticed.

As she made her way up the stairs toward Muffy's suite, she reviewed the conversation she and McPhee had been having just prior to the kiss. They'd been talking about her getting a job, her interest in renewable energy, volunteer work, how useless and spoiled she was. None of those topics seemed particularly provocative.

What, then? She didn't have a clue.

Muffy's door was partially opened, so Sonya tapped on it. "Mother?"

"Come in, dear!" Muffy said cheerfully. She was sitting cross-legged on the bed, wearing a pair of loose, gauzy pants and a matching shirt. She did not look like a woman who'd recently spent a month in the hospital.

Scattered all around Muffy were several CDs. She had a portable CD player in her lap and earbuds in her ears.

"I was just listening to the different songs the Brent

Warren Orchestra can play for your reception. Now I've made a list of the ones I like, but I want you to listen to all of them and make up your own list, keeping in mind the running times and the fact that we'll have approximately three hours to fill. We'll see where our lists agree and where they diverge. Of course, you get to make the final decision—"

"Mother, I'm sure your choices will be fine."

"You're going to be on the plane for hours, anyway. You might as well listen to something nice." She gathered up the CDs into a stack and handed them to Sonya, who dutifully took them along with the player.

"All right." She supposed there were more stressful things Muffy could do than listen to orchestral music. But she wished her mother wouldn't get so wigged out about every tiny detail. If it were Sonya's decision, she would just let the orchestra play whatever they normally played at weddings. But it wasn't her decision, no matter what Muffy said.

"You look a bit strange, dear," Muffy said, examining Sonya's face carefully. "You're not coming down with something, are you?"

Only insanity. "No, I feel great."

"Take some extra vitamin C. You know, planes are just breeding grounds for all kinds of diseases. All that recirculated air."

"Speaking of vitamins, have you taken your morning medications?"

"Yes, dear."

"And will you promise me not to argue with Matilda about the food? She's working with the nutritionist on some more interesting dishes, but it might take a while."

"I'll try to be good," Muffy said. "You just go and have fun. Take your time with Madame Boirot, and make sure you're really in love with the lace before you commit."

Sonya thought guiltily about the way she'd just chosen a pattern at random before ordering. "I will."

Muffy reached under her pillow and withdrew some cash. She handed it to Sonya. "Use this to buy something for John-Michael. A really nice gift. I haven't thanked him properly for saving my life."

Sonya eyed the stack of cash with a practiced eye. It was about five hundred dollars. She could hardly refuse to carry out Muffy's wishes, not when the gesture was so generous, and borne out of gratitude. And much as she'd like to, she couldn't get away with buying a joke gift or something bland and impersonal. Muffy would find out.

"Are you sure you're okay?" Muffy asked, sounding genuinely concerned. "When you came in you were pale as a mist, and now you're flushed."

"I'm fine. I better go before we miss our plane."

WHEN SONYA CAME DOWNSTAIRS, McPhee was waiting in the foyer for her. He'd already brought her sporty little BMW around to the front. It was doubtless sparkling clean and full of gas. Tim always took care of stuff like that for her.

Oh, Lord, she was spoiled.

"I hope you don't mind if I put on my earphones,"

she said once they'd settled into the car, trying to restore some sense of normalcy between them. "My mother has given me an assignment. I have to pick out music for the reception." She indicated the stack of CDs and the portable player, which she'd tucked into a Louis Vuitton tote bag. She was grateful she had the task, because she didn't feel she could handle making small talk with McPhee for four hours. Her body was still vibrating from that kiss. She needed some quiet time to process what had happened and formulate a plan for how she would deal with it.

"No problem. I have some thinking to do myself."

Now that just made her curious. Would he be thinking about their kiss? Or had he already dismissed their encounter and moved on to something more practical, like choosing a new health insurance plan or whether to hire a moving company for when he moved out of his apartment above the Pattersons' garage?

Chapter Five

By the time the BMW had cleared the Patterson drive-way, Sonya had the CD player's earphones on, but she didn't listen to any music. It would only make her depressed. She perused her mother's list, crossed off three songs she didn't like. "Disco Duck"? Even if this wedding had been relegated to the abstract, no one was playing "Disco Duck" at her reception. She replaced the three with jazz songs she knew she would enjoy, were she to ever hear them.

Her task was completed, and they weren't even out of her neighborhood yet.

She pulled a glossy magazine from her tote and flipped through it. But she found she couldn't concentrate on the latest designer fashions or trendy weekend getaway destinations. There was no getting around it. She had to consider what had just happened between her and McPhee, deal with it, put it in a box in her mind, shut the lid tight, and forget about it.

Unlike the painful and embarrassing incident ten years ago, this time McPhee had initiated the kiss. After all, it couldn't have been her. She'd been spitting mad, her pride bruised by McPhee's refusal to immediately embrace the idea that she should get a job and become a more productive member of society. She'd been intent on getting him to confess he thought her too spoiled, stupid or lazy to work. She hadn't been thinking about kissing or sex or anything the least bit scandalous…had she?

But she sure hadn't fought off McPhee. She hadn't put up even token resistance. So maybe somewhere, in the back of her mind, she'd been thinking of something other than her job qualifications.

For a few minutes she let herself experience the kiss again, the feel of McPhee's big hands on her body, tangled in her hair, the warmth of his mouth against hers, the taste of blueberries on his tongue, the smell of his sun-bronzed skin, the beating of his heart against her chest.

She hadn't been able to remember much about the first time they'd kissed. She'd been tipsy on margaritas, and in the morning her most vivid recollection had been the sting of McPhee's rejection, not the feel of his body pressed against hers.

This morning's kiss was different.

She went through it again, recalling particulars, even such inconsequential details as the gurgle of the coffeepot in the background and the feel of the corded muscles in his neck.

The memories were sweet torture. Her body responded, almost as if she were experiencing the kiss for real. She squirmed in her seat, then turned the thermostat on the climate control down to sixty-five degrees. She was having a hot flash!

She caught McPhee's gaze and realized he was watching her. For how long? Her face flamed at the possibility that he'd been watching long enough to catch the play of emotions that must have crossed her face.

She removed the headphones. "Did you want to say something?"

"Sonya, we have to talk."

"I'm…I'm not ready to talk."

"Then just let me do the talking. I'm very sorry about what hap— No, that's not right. It didn't just happen. I made it happen. It was very wrong of me, and believe me, it won't—"

Sonya didn't hear the rest. She'd put the earphones back on and hit the play button.

"Hey! I'm apologizing here!"

But she didn't want to hear an apology. She realized with no small shock that what she wanted him to say was that he *wasn't* sorry, that it *wasn't* a big mistake, that he'd enjoyed it and wanted to do it again.

Impossible! She couldn't function while such ridiculous thoughts were rambling around her brain. These feelings were simply the residual emotions from an adolescent crush that she'd never dealt with properly.

She did what she'd always done when dealing with her unrequited crush on McPhee. She wrapped herself with cold indignation and reminded herself of her mother's advice: *Never let them see you cry.*

She removed the earphones. "I accept your apology, and I offer one of my own," she said primly. "Apparently I provoked you into an animalistic display of dominant behavior. When you couldn't dredge an answer to my perfectly reasonable question from your pea-size brain, you did what most males do when confronted with a situation they can't handle at an intellectual level—you responded physically."

"Um, that didn't sound like much of an apology."

"It was the best I could come up with. I don't really think I did anything wrong, but I was trying to be polite."

"What was the question you asked? The one that was too intellectually challenging for my pea brain?"

"We were discussing whether you thought I could handle a job. And though you didn't say it, I got the distinct impression you thought the idea ludicrous."

"Sonya, I believe you could do anything you put your mind to. And that's the God's honest truth. I don't think you're stupid or lazy."

Was he patronizing her? She had to admit he seemed sincere this time. No smirk, no laughter in his eyes.

"Watch the road," she said, then put the earphones back on. Oh, Lord, how was she going to spend two days with him? At least she'd be with Cindy and Brenna soon. Having others around would provide a welcome buffer.

JOHN-MICHAEL DIDN'T KNOW what else to do about that illicit kiss. They'd talked about it; he'd apologized; she'd accepted his apology; he was determined it wouldn't happen again. But the matter felt…unfinished.

Well, of course it does. It wouldn't be finished until

he and Sonya made love. What were the chances? Yesterday, he'd have said zero. But he kept thinking about the way she'd responded, and wondering how different the dynamics of their relationship would be once he was no longer her bodyguard.

They didn't talk at all until he drove across the city limits of Cottonwood, Texas. It was a quaint little town, and driving through it felt like stepping back in time fifty years. It still had a full-service gas station. And a dime-store.

He tapped her on the arm. She jumped and pulled off the headphones. "This is where you spent two weeks of your life?"

"Yes. You find that hard to believe?"

"Where did you get your nails done?" Sonya was religious about having her acrylic nails filled and polished every two weeks.

"At the Clip 'n' Snip." She pointed to a storefront with a pink awning and a giant pair of neon scissors in the window. "They have a great manicurist there."

He should have known she wouldn't spend time anywhere there wasn't a beauty shop.

"Go all around the square to the opposite corner. The Kountry Kozy B&B is that purple Victorian house."

"Saints preserve us," he mumbled, doing an imitation of Jock. "Do I actually have to stay at this place?"

"There's a motel in Mooresville, across the lake, if you'd rather. I think it's called the Stay-and-Pay."

"You want to get rid of me that bad?"

She shrugged. "You're the one complaining about the accommodations."

She was still mad at him, though he wasn't sure why. The kiss? Or was she still steamed about the way he'd reacted when she announced she wanted to get a job? He couldn't stand two days of this. He had to get things back to normal with them.

Back to normal? What was normal? She was being cool and detached; he was being faintly mocking. That *was* normal. Or, at least, it had been normal for the past ten years. He didn't want to go back to that. He wanted to see more of the friendly, funny Sonya.

He realized then that somewhere in the back of his mind he'd been hoping things would change when he told her he was leaving his job as her bodyguard—that they could move forward rather than backward. Maybe that's what the kiss was about. He was already living with one foot in the future, when he would be a free agent, a deputy sheriff, no longer merely the gardener's son. And Sonya Patterson would be fair game, no longer his boss's daughter.

His father would say he was kidding himself. Jock would point out that John-Michael would never be on Sonya's social or economic level no matter how much he excelled in his new career. But Jock was from a different generation. In the twenty-first century, class distinctions weren't so rigidly drawn.

Were they?

He parked in front of the huge house, which dripped with lacy fretwork and curlicues, and went to the back of the car to get their bags out of the trunk. Sonya, meanwhile, got out and headed up a walkway toward the house, confident her needs would be taken care of.

She'd probably never carried her own suitcase in her life. He wondered if she'd conned Cindy or Brenna into toting her things when The Blondes were traveling together.

Before Sonya reached the wrap-around porch, the front door burst open and Cindy Lefler Rheems flew out, her honey-blond hair streaming behind her. She had on faded jeans and a Miracle Café sweatshirt.

"Sonya! It's so great to see you!" She and Sonya embraced warmly. Cindy threw her whole body into the hug. And the odd thing was, Sonya did, too. This was nothing like the polite, stiff little hugs she gave her other friends, accompanied by air kisses near the cheek. These two had genuine affection for each other.

As the two women separated, Cindy's gaze lit on the BMW. "What, no limo this time? Hi, McPhee!"

He gave her a nod and a wave.

Cindy then whispered something to Sonya while looking straight at John Michael.

Sonya whispered something back and rolled her eyes.

John-Michael looked away, not wanting to think about what Sonya might be telling her friend about him. Had he become the servant who had an impossible crush on her? Or was he merely the overprotective bodyguard, a role he was used to playing? Would she tell her friends about the kiss, downplaying her response?

She might be able to get away with that among her friends, but he knew better. At some point she was going to have to acknowledge the tension thrumming between them. Not now, when she had a sick mother, a runaway wedding and an AWOL fiancé.

But soon.

"SO, WHAT'S GOING ON with you and the hunky bodyguard?" Cindy asked. They were ensconced in their old room at the B&B, waiting for Brenna to arrive. McPhee had wisely retired to his own room down the hall. "I mean, I've never asked you this, but what's it like to *have* a bodyguard?"

"Annoying, most of the time."

"Does he go on dates with you?"

"I can't date my bodyguard," Sonya said, alarmed that Cindy had picked up on the residual sexual vibes between herself and McPhee.

"I meant, when you date somebody else, does he have to come along?"

"Oh. He follows discreetly behind, usually in another car. I managed to lose him a couple of times when I was in college, but he always found me, so I gave up trying. When I was running around Texas and Louisiana with you and Brenna, that was the first time I'd given him the slip in ten years."

"So you were, like, a fugitive?"

Sonya grinned at her friend. "It was wonderful."

"So why don't you fire him?"

"He's on my mother's payroll, not mine. She insists. And if it stops her from worrying, I guess I can put up with it. Though I won't have to for long. He's got another job, starting in January, right after my supposed wedding date."

"You must be happy about that." Cindy watched her carefully.

"I'll be very pleased to see the last of him," Sonya said breezily.

"Is he that awful?"

"Beastly."

"Is that why you're so mean to him?"

Sonya sat up straighter. "Mean?"

"Well, I couldn't help noticing that you didn't say a word to him."

"I've known him all my life," Sonya said, uncomfortably aware of Cindy's scrutiny. None of Sonya's other friends had ever questioned the way she treated her bodyguard. He was an employee, after all. "We don't normally have a lot to say to each other."

"What does he do that's beastly?" Cindy wanted to know. "Does he curse or drink? Make lewd comments? Scratch himself?"

"No, of course not. He's just…got an attitude," she finished lamely.

"You mean, he's not properly deferential?"

"No, I don't mean that!" Sonya said, getting riled, until she realized Cindy was deliberately baiting her. She didn't know Cindy quite as well as she knew Brenna, but she'd observed that Cindy treated everyone as an equal, from the mayor down to the lowliest busboy working at her café. She'd had a net worth of almost a million dollars before Marvin had wiped her out, yet no one in town had even realized it.

"I'm just trying to understand," Cindy said as she pulled the cork on a bottle of white wine. "I'd have to be blind and deaf not to feel the weird vibes going on between you two."

"We had a disagreement this morning, that's all," Sonya said. "He apologized, I apologized." Of course, her apology had been sarcastic and insincere, when she knew darn well she'd been a willing participant in that kiss. "Things are just still a bit tense between us. But we'll get over it. I'm actually very fond of McPhee. We often argue about things, but we forgive and forget."

"Do you always call him McPhee?"

"Well, yes. I guess I do." His first name felt far too intimate.

"Does avoiding his first name help maintain a proper distance?"

"Cindy! I've always called him McPhee." But, no, that wasn't true. She'd switched to calling him by his last name after he'd rejected her advances. It *had* helped her maintain distance.

"What's his first name?" Cindy asked.

"John-Michael. Well, that's his first and middle. Like any good southern boy, he goes by both."

"What does he call you?"

"He calls me Sonya. Now stop interrogating me."

Cindy softened. "All right. But if you ever want to talk about it—"

"Why would I want to talk about my bodyguard?"

"Because I think you're in love with him. And before you sputter your denials, let me remind you that I know about these things. How long did I spend denying I was in love with Luke? We were childhood sweethearts, but I tossed him away because I thought there was no way to breach the differences between us. But there's always a way."

Sonya was so stunned she couldn't speak. Cindy had gone right to the heart of it. Maybe she did still have feelings for McPhee, and not just "residual" ones. But the barriers between them were so huge, their history so complex, the layers of hurt and resentment so deep, she couldn't really put a name to how she felt about him, or them.

She was horrified when tears sprang to her eyes.

"Oh, honey, I didn't mean to make you cry."

Sonya laughed, swallowing back the tears before they could get out of hand. "And I thought Brenna was the frank, outspoken one of The Blondes." She found a tissue, dabbed at her eyes, then got out her compact and repaired the damage to her makeup. She could easily turn into a narcissist if she wasn't careful. Her whole life, she'd been accustomed to having her every need met by maids, cooks, store clerks and anyone else who might benefit financially from her goodwill. Those few weeks she'd spent traveling around with Brenna, where no one knew she was Muffy Patterson's daughter, had been an eye opener.

Everyone really *wasn't* interested in her simply because she was wonderful and special. For the first time in her life, she'd been anonymous. Not that she hadn't enjoyed her anonymity somewhat, but she'd learned something about what she'd taken for granted all her life. Not just being able to buy anything she wanted, but the way everyone treated her.

"So, did you bring your honeymoon pictures this

time?" Sonya asked briskly. The last time they'd gotten together, Cindy hadn't yet developed her film from Italy. "I want to see every detail of the trip. Well, no," she added quickly, "not *every* detail." The two women laughed, and Sonya relaxed, hoping the subject of her relationship with McPhee was closed.

JOHN-MICHAEL HAD JUST SETTLED into a leather club chair—his room wasn't nearly as ruffly and flowery as he'd feared it would be—and cracked open a book when he heard feminine squeals. Brenna had arrived, apparently. He tried to concentrate, but the high-pitched laughter and softer murmurs distracted him terribly. Here he was again, sitting on the outside while Sonya lived her life. Usually the isolation of his position didn't get to him, but just now it did. He should have been grateful to be left alone with his mystery novel, but he wasn't.

To his surprise, someone tapped on his door a few minutes later. He stood to open it, expecting a housekeeper with towels or something. Instead he found Cindy. "We're going over to the Miracle Café for lunch. Do you want to come with us?"

"I'll grab something later," he said automatically. He recalled that Brenna and Cindy had tried to include him a few times during the weekend in Dallas, but he'd resisted then, too.

"We could really use your input," she said. "Sonya told us you have a degree in criminology, and you've been through the police academy. Maybe you'll have some insight into Marvin's personality."

He had to confess, he was tempted. What man wouldn't want to share a meal with three gorgeous blondes? But Sonya would probably glare at him the whole time.

"Sonya and I spend a lot of time together," he said. "I imagine she would prefer it if I stay invisible."

"This isn't India," Cindy huffed. "We don't have a caste system."

Clearly Cindy hadn't hung around Houston high society much, or she would know that there definitely was a caste system. Unspoken, but rigid as the wrought-iron fences that surround the millionaires' estates.

"I have some things I need to take care of," he said. "But thanks for inviting me."

"Well, all right. I guess we can pick your brain later when we're at my house."

"What?"

But she turned and walked away.

John-Michael resumed his seat by the window, where he had a clear view of the Miracle Café. Keeping an eye on Sonya's activities was such an ingrained activity, he did it even when there was no conceivable danger to her. He couldn't think of a safer place than this friendly little town.

When a second knock sounded on his door, He opened it more warily. This time Heath Packer was leaning against the door frame.

"Hey." John-Michael offered his hand, and Heath took it. He and the former FBI agent, now a private investigator, had been forced to get to know each other during the last "blonde reunion," but they'd first met in the closet of a New Orleans hotel room, when they'd both been caught in the middle of an illegal search. "I understand congratulations are in order."

Heath smiled without even a trace of chagrin. "Yup. Brenna's making an honest man out of me."

"I didn't know you would be here."

"The last time Brenna went after Marvin, she nearly broke her neck jumping down an empty elevator shaft. I intend to keep an eye on things."

John-Michael let Heath into his room, and the two of them stood at the window for a few silent moments. "It's a knee-jerk reaction for men to try to protect women."

"The caveman in us," Heath agreed.

"When you stop and think about it, The Blondes do a pretty good job of taking care of themselves. The three of them together are kind of scary. I wouldn't want them coming after *me*."

"Yeah, Marvin's probably the one who needs protecting."

They laughed.

"Seriously, though," John-Michael said, "does it strike you as a little bit odd, the way those three women became such fast friends so quickly?"

"Crime victims often bond in a way no one else can understand," Heath said. "I've seen it before." He looked critically around the small, impeccably decorated bedroom. "I hope you're not going to spend the whole weekend in here. Luke Rheems, Cindy's husband, said we could come on over for a beer."

Now Cindy's cryptic comment made sense. And

John-Michael had to admit, a beer with the guys sounded like a great idea. Sonya was safe eating at Cindy's café, for at least a while.

AT LUKE'S HOUSE they ordered pizza, drank beer, watched college football and talked about cars, guns and sports—and kept an eye on Cindy's little boy, who at sixteen months was into everything. It was the sort of male bonding John-Michael had done little of over the past few years, trapped in the insular World of Patterson, and it felt good.

But after a couple of beers, he felt a little melancholy, too. When Luke and Heath had had enough of drinking, swearing and eating high-fat junk food, they had women to come home to, comfortable domesticity to fall back on. Luke had nothing.

Maybe he'd get a dog, he thought, scratching the Rheems's black lab puppy behind her ears. She was sweet, loyal, uncomplicated.

"So shouldn't we be the ones going after Marvin Carter?" John-Michael asked suddenly. "You two have law enforcement experience, and I've at least got some training."

"Yeah, but we're not scorned women," Luke pointed out.

Heath grinned. "Can't discount that factor." But then he sobered. "Don't worry, McPhee. When the girls get here in a while, they'll bring us into the loop. Law enforcement has failed them in the past, but they're not too proud to accept our help if we offer it. And I'm by-god-sure going to offer it and not take no for an answer."

"Damn straight," John-Michael couldn't help saying. He hadn't planned on letting Sonya run off on her mission of revenge without some professional backup, but he was relieved to know he would have help. He wondered if Sonya was as keen to include him as the others seemed to be. Or would he be invisible to her, the way he'd been whenever she socialized with her old friends back in Houston? He was determined that she see him as something other than the ubiquitous bodyguard.

AT THE MIRACLE CAFÉ, Sonya ordered an incredibly unhealthy meal of pot roast, mashed potatoes with gravy, creamed corn and apple cobbler, reveling in the fat grams and the companionship. Several people who remembered Sonya and Brenna from when they'd visited Cottonwood weeks earlier stopped by their table and said hi.

"I just love your hair," said Margie Blankenship, referring to Brenna's platinum spikes. Margie worked at the real estate office.

"Really?" Brenna said. "I was thinking how cool your hair is. Very retro."

"Oh, aren't you sweet." Margie patted her impressive beehive. "Y'all come out to the Red Dog later if you want to kick up your heels."

Sonya marveled at the small-town friendliness. During her first visit, they'd been outsiders, but now the townspeople treated them like old friends. She used to wonder how people in small towns could stand it, but life here in Cottonwood didn't seem to be so bad.

"I'm thinking about getting a job," Sonya said once they'd gotten the initial catching up out of the way.

Brenna couldn't completely stifle her snort of disbelief.

"Oh, not you too!" Sonya felt betrayed. "John-Michael doesn't think I'm cut out to earn my own living."

"Sorry," Brenna said quickly. "I know you could do just about anything, and I'm the last person who should laugh about a rich girl wanting to do something with her life and become self-sufficient. Lord knows I've taken enough heat from my family about my jewelry business."

"Then why *did* you laugh?" Sonya asked. She asked the question without any animosity. She truly wanted to know.

"Well," Brenna answered with equal candor, "I guess it's the first impression you made with me. Your clothes, your hair, your nails—they scream 'rich society girl.'"

"Can't a working woman be well-groomed?" Sonya asked, looking down at herself. She'd always taken pride in her clothing and accessories, and had thought that was a good thing.

Cindy answered. "Most working girls don't have the time for more than a reasonable level of hygiene and style. Throw kids, a husband and a house into the mix, and I'm lucky to get a bath every day. Not that I'm complaining!"

"So you're saying I'm…"

"High maintenance," Brenna confirmed. "So, is that why you're mad at your bodyguard? He implied you didn't have the right stuff?"

Sonya didn't want to get into that subject again. "Let's just say he's irritated me on a number of levels today. Back to this 'high-maintenance' theory. You're saying I have an image problem?"

"I wouldn't say it's a problem." Brenna covertly inspected Sonya's manicure. "I would love to be as well put together as you. Even among your usual peer group, you probably set the bar."

"My usual peer group, being those rich snotty sorority girls I hang with?"

"Exactly," Brenna said, not even realizing she'd just insulted Sonya. "But if you want to do something with your life, I totally applaud you. Doing something you love is better than all the cash at Fort Knox. What sort of work is it you think you'd like to do?"

"Engineering," Sonya said eagerly, "particularly in the areas of alternative energy sources. Maybe designing more efficient wind turbines or solar panels."

Her two friends went completely still. "Engineering?" they said together.

"Yes! That's what my degree is in. Chemical engineering, to be exact, with the idea that I would go into some facet of the oil business, because that's what my father did. But I took a lot of classes in mechanical and environmental engineering, too."

"Hmm," Brenna said, sharing a look with Cindy. "We knew you had some awesome computer skills, but you never mentioned engineering before." The skeptical looks on their faces were priceless.

"Oh, I give up," Sonya said with a laugh. There was no reason to take herself so seriously. They could all sit up and take notice when she actually did get a job. Until then, well, she didn't exactly have a track record that inspired confidence in her abilities. "Someday I'm going to invent something really awesome that will change your life, and you'll be sorry you made fun of me."

She eyed the last bite of her cobbler and decided to leave it on the plate. Her pants felt tight enough as it was. "I feel so guilty. My mother's at home eating all this horrible-tasting health food, and I'm gorging on enough fat and carbohydrates to feed a football team."

"Indulging every once in a while won't hurt," Cindy chided her. Cindy hadn't exactly held back, munching down fried chicken and french fries. "I only eat here once a week myself, and I own the place."

"I wondered why you weren't the size of a '56 Chevy," Sonya said.

"I burn off the fat chasing after a highly ambulatory sixteen-month-old."

"I don't want to hear any diet talk," said Brenna, who had such a fast metabolism she could eat whatever she wanted all the time and maintain her cute, curvy little figure. Currently, she was polishing off a hot fudge sundae.

As the meal wound down, Sonya grabbed her purse and started to pull out some money, but Cindy stopped her. "Don't you dare. After all the stuff you paid for when Brenna and I were broke, are you kidding? This is my treat."

"All right, all right." As she rearranged her little purse so she could squeeze her wallet back inside, a wad of bills fell out on the table.

Brenna picked it up. "Good Lord, that's enough cash to stop up a bathtub drain."

"It's not mine," Sonya said, quickly reclaiming the money. "My mother gave it to me. I'm supposed to use it to buy a gift for John-Michael."

"Is it his birthday?" Cindy asked.

"No. He saved my mother's life by getting her to the hospital when she had her heart attack. The gift is supposed to be a thank-you from her. But I have no idea what to buy for him. Maybe you all can help me."

"Hmm, I can think of a few things he might like," Brenna said, arching one speculative eyebrow.

Cindy nudged Brenna under the table. "Stop teasing Sonya. She needs our help." Cindy returned her attention to Sonya. "What does he like?"

"Cars and motorcycles. Guns."

Cindy and Brenna wrinkled their noses. "What else?" Brenna asked.

Sonya tried, but she couldn't think of anything else.

"And you've known this man how long?" Cindy asked.

"Since I was born," Sonya admitted. He knew virtually every detail of her life—or he had, until recently. She knew very little about his. She tried to think back to when they were kids. What were his interests then? Had he ever had hobbies? Cars, motorcycles, guns and heavy-metal music, that was all she could remember.

Then a fuzzy recollection popped into her head, becoming clearer as she tried to focus in on it.

"What?" Cindy and Brenna asked together.

"He liked to look at the stars," she said. "The sky

isn't very clear in Houston, but sometimes, in the winter, you'll be able to see the stars. I remember he had this itty-bitty telescope, and he would go up on the roof with it...." And suddenly she knew what she would buy John-Michael with Muffy's five hundred dollars. No matter how he aggravated her, she and her mother owed him, and she *would* get him a gift that meant something, damn it.

"SO YOU'VE ACTUALLY TALKED to his parents?" Heath asked John-Michael. "They wouldn't say a damn thing to me." They were all six seated around the Rheems's dining room table, comparing notes on what they each knew about Marvin Carter and floating theories about how to force him to surface. Sonya was seated to John-Michael's immediate left, close enough at the small table that he could smell her light perfume. Cindy had taken pains to seat everyone where she wanted them, causing him to wonder if she might be trying to play matchmaker. He wasn't against the idea, though at this point it was premature. He had a few weeks to go before he could pursue Sonya.

"Maybe the Carters weren't as intimidated by me," John-Michael said, forcing himself to focus on the business at hand. "Since I'm not law enforcement. Anyway, they're pretty fed up with their darling son at this point. They've been protecting him from the consequences of his actions for years, looking the other way when he stole from them. But now they're ready to let him take the fall. I even thought of going up there to talk to them. They claim they don't know where he is, but maybe they could figure it out, if we asked the right questions."

"That's a great idea," Brenna said. "Who's up for a trip to Boston? We could talk to his parents, then hit up Marvin's old friends from high school, his neighbors."

"I'll go," Cindy immediately said. Cindy apparently never turned down the opportunity to travel. "Maybe Marvin's parents will feel sorry for me, since I'm one of their son's victims and I have a small child."

"I'm in," Heath said.

Luke laughed. "Must be nice to be your own boss. I could probably swing a couple of days, but I'll have to work out my schedule."

Cindy nudged him. "You can get off. You've never been to Boston, have you?"

"I hardly ever left Cottonwood until you started dragging me all over the place." But there was only fondness in his voice.

Brenna looked at Sonya and raised a questioning eyebrow.

"I'd love to go, but it will depend on how my mother is doing."

"And she does have a wedding to plan," John-Michael couldn't resist adding. He hoped the others would convince her that it was time to tell her mother the truth.

Cindy's eyes widened. "Oh, Sonya, you've got to be kidding."

"I can't tell my mother the wedding's off," Sonya said a bit desperately. "She'll have another heart attack and die. You all have no idea how much she's counting on this wedding. Her doctor says it's therapeutic. I can't take that away from her."

"But, Sonya," Brenna said, her voice uncharacteristically gentle. "The longer you wait—"

"I know, I know. The worse it will be. But surely a little longer won't hurt. Just until she's a little stronger."

Her friends grudgingly agreed that she was probably a better judge of what her mother could and couldn't handle, and they left her alone.

The group decided on a trip to Boston in two weeks, provided Luke could work out his schedule. Sonya was itching to go, John-Michael could tell. "Surely in two weeks…" She left the sentence unfinished.

"What about you, John-Michael?" Brenna asked. "You've already established some level of trust with the Carters. Your participation would be invaluable."

"You should go," Sonya said to him, "even if I can't."

The idea of taking a trip out of town without Sonya seemed downright weird. But he'd better get used to doing things without her. His last day as her bodyguard was fast approaching. Even if they got into a relationship—and that was a big if—they would no longer be attached at the hip. "I'll go," he said, and when the women applauded his decision—physically applauded—he felt a warm sense of inclusion.

No wonder Sonya had bonded so quickly with these women—and, now, with their men. They were good people, and they did treat her like regular folks. Around them, John-Michael felt he could see more of Sonya as she really was, without the layers of protection her money and position normally afforded her.

And again he felt more and more drawn to her, more and more certain that he couldn't let her just slip out of his life completely without a fight.

THAT NIGHT they all went country dancing at a place called the Red Dog Saloon. Sonya found it delightfully tacky, the sort of place she wouldn't have set foot in a few weeks ago.

Cindy taught them how to do the Cotton-Eyed Joe and the Texas two-step, and even when Sonya's friends manipulated her into dancing with John-Michael a couple of times, she didn't mind. She made a show of pretending to be put out, but she totally enjoyed the feeling of John-Michael's arms around her, especially when they did a fast polka. Sonya's steps were often wildly out of control, and during the Orange Blossom Special, John-Michael had to hold her close to keep her from annihilating other couples on the dance floor.

Abruptly the music changed to a slow country ballad, and Sonya felt a tremendous urge to lay her head against John-Michael's shoulder and just let him keep holding her while she caught her breath. Their eyes locked, and she knew he was thinking the same thing. Their kiss that morning hadn't been a fluke. The chemistry between them wasn't going away.

But chemistry didn't always lead to anything lasting, Sonya reminded herself.

It was John-Michael who gently set her away from him. "Want me to get you another beer?"

Nice, safe territory, she thought dazedly. John-Michael, the dutiful employee, seeing to her comfort.

"No, thanks," she murmured. Her brain was fogged enough. Did he, or did he not want her? And if he did, what held him back? If it was just his employment situation, that would be ending soon enough. Was he merely waiting? Or were there other reasons? Other women?

THEY LEFT COTTONWOOD after dinner on Sunday. After many hugs and promises to stay in touch, Sonya, exhausted and talked out, reclined her seat, thinking she would snooze most of the way back to Houston. She didn't trust herself, alone in a dark car with John-Michael.

"Did you have a good time?" John-Michael asked.

"Do you need to ask? I should send Marvin a thank-you note for picking such great women to fleece."

"He does have good taste," John-Michael agreed. Though Sonya knew he was just being a guy, and guys appreciated pretty women, she felt a twinge of jealousy that he found her friends attractive. "So," he added, "are you done being mad at me?"

"It takes too much energy staying mad at you," she said with a sigh.

"Then you should be exhausted. You've been mad at me for ten years."

"That's not—" The denial died abirthing. It was true. She had been mad at him for ten years. And all because he had spurned her sexual advances. Despite her assurances that she'd put the incident behind her, it wasn't true. In some ways she was still that insecure nineteen-year-old, looking for some sign that John-Michael returned her growing feelings.

And when she didn't find it, the temptation to freeze him out was strong. But that was an immature girl's response, and she was determined not to hold it against John-Michael if he didn't want to get involved with her, whatever his reasons.

"If you're serious about getting a job," he said, "I'll help any way I can."

Oh, that. "I guess I shouldn't have gotten mad at you over the job thing. Brenna and Cindy proved your reaction was a universal one. They laughed, too. But I am serious," she added. Then she thought to ask, "Does it bother you that I call you by your last name? Cindy seemed to think it was demeaning."

He shrugged. "It's what I'm used to. John-Michael is quite a mouthful."

She wished he wouldn't say "John-Michael" and "mouthful" in the same sentence. It made her think of something he probably never intended. "But do you like it?" she persisted.

He paused before answering. "No. I liked it better when you called me by my given name. But I was the one who slammed the door on getting too familiar, so I guess I can't complain."

"You sure flung that door open again yesterday morning."

"I've apologized for—"

"I'm not looking for an apology. I'm looking for answers. It's taken me a while, but I understand why you weren't interested in me when I was nineteen. I was immature and spoiled. I was used to guys jumping through hoops for me, standing at attention when I snapped my fingers. I expected you to do the same. But you weren't some callow prep school boy I could play like a fiddle. I was probably incredibly boring to you."

"That's a very pretty analysis," McPhee said. "But the truth of the matter is, you were my boss's daughter. I was being paid to protect you, not debauch you. Muffy would have had me drawn and quartered if I'd touched a hair on your head, and my father would have been out on the street. If you'd been anyone else, I'd have had you between the sheets so fast your head would still be spinning."

Chapter Six

John-Michael wondered if he'd gone a little too far. He glanced over at Sonya, who looked like she'd been pole-axed. Could an event that took place ten years ago really matter so much to her now?

He flashed her a regretful grin. "You wanted me to be honest, right?"

"So it was all an act?" she squeaked. "You weren't really repulsed by me? You didn't really think I was a spoiled brat?"

"You *were* spoiled. But that's something I could have overlooked under other circumstances."

He never saw it coming. One minute Sonya was sitting in the passenger seat looking dazed. The next, her fist was heading for him at supersonic speed. Fortunately, she aimed for his arm rather than his face, or the car might have ended up in a ditch.

"Ow!" He rubbed the offended muscle. Where had she learned how to pack such a wallop? At Muffy's insistence, Sonya had taken self-defense classes a few years ago, some martial arts thing. John-Michael had always sat out in the parking lot rather than observe her class, figuring he didn't need to watch Sonya rolling around on mats with brawny pseudo-assailants. It would have only made him wish he could join in the fun. "So what was that for?"

"All this time, you let me think you hated and despised me, that you were repulsed and disgusted and amused by my pathetic romantic overture. You said all those mean things. I bet you even made up the girlfriend!"

"Oh, yeah, the girlfriend."

"Well, did you? Have one?"

"I have dated a few women over the years." But not too seriously. They always got turned off by his single-minded devotion to keeping Sonya safe, and he never fought too hard to keep them.

"But did you have a girlfriend that night? Or were you lying?"

"I don't remember."

The look Sonya gave him made her seem suddenly dangerous. Her green eyes were bright and narrowed like a cat's, her succulent lips ever so slightly curled.

"All right, no, I wasn't dating anyone seriously at that time."

She folded her arms and leaned back in her seat, staring out at the oncoming headlights as their car hurtled through the night. "You could have just told me the truth. It wouldn't have hurt so much. I had feelings for you. Maybe it was just a girlish crush, but it felt very real to me. You hurt me."

The naked honesty in those three words got to him.

They'd played a lot of games over the years, danced around the issues, alternately shown each other hostility or cool detachment. But they'd seldom been honest.

"I know I did," he said. "I hurt you on purpose."

"Why?" The anguish in her voice almost undid him.

"It was the only way, Sonya. If I'd told you the truth, that I really did want you, you'd have found a way to talk me into making love with you. I wouldn't have resisted too hard. I had to break it off clean, or we'd have wound up in bed. And that would have led to nowhere but disaster."

"How can you be so sure?"

"Sonya. You were a debutante, an oil heiress, destined to be one of the richest women in the state of Texas. I was the son of an alcoholic Irish immigrant. Do the math. It would never have worked, even in the short term."

"We live in America," she grumbled. But she didn't take that argument any further, probably because she knew as well as he did that her starry-eyed fantasies of ten years ago had been unrealistic.

They rode in silence for the next hour or so. Sonya put in a CD—not one with wedding music, thank God. It was something she'd found in the glove compartment, a female blues singer who had died before either John-Michael or Sonya had been born. The music seemed to suit their collective mood.

Closer to Houston, the traffic became stop-and-go as it almost always did, even in nonpeak hours.

"I appreciate you doing all the driving," Sonya said, breaking the silence. "But I really should spend more time behind the wheel. It's embarrassing that I let myself get so dependent on you and Tim for my transportation." She paused, a pensive expression on her face. "I can't cook, either."

"You can do a valve job on a '67 Mustang," John-Michael reminded her. He'd taught her to do that himself, back when she'd been fifteen or so, following him around like a puppy.

She smiled, the first time she'd done so since they'd left Cottonwood. "That's true, I can. I don't know that that's a particularly useful skill, given that no one drives those old cars anymore, but I am handy with a wrench. Do you want to hear something really sad?"

"Do I?"

"This morning, Brenna asked me to fix coffee in the little coffee pot that was in our room. I didn't know how. I thought she was going to rupture something laughing at me."

"And she's your friend?"

"Yes, she is my friend. She sees me as an elitist, high-maintenance snob who does not have the survival skills—or the intelligence—of a gnat, but she loves me anyway. Look what she gave me." She held up her wrist, which was graced by a silver chain bearing one tiny charm. "It's a tiny bottle of nail polish. When we were traveling together, she always gave me a hard time about my nails. She made this specially, just for me, because I helped her get her jewelry ready for the New York show. That's a friend."

John-Michael thought Sonya's enthusiasm over her new trinket was endearing. She hadn't been that excited over her four-carat engagement ring from Marvin, even when she'd still believed it was a real diamond.

Sonya was surprising him at every turn these days. He wondered how many more surprises he could stand. Right before his eyes, she was transforming from his ideal-woman fantasy prototype into a real-live, flesh-and-blood woman who was becoming more and more difficult to resist.

It hadn't escaped his attention that, during their frank conversation earlier, one question had gone unasked, and it was a doozy. Did he still feel the same about her as he had ten years ago? Or had he gotten over it?

A few weeks ago, he could have answered yes, that he'd moved on. Now he wasn't so sure. Those old feelings had sneaked up on him, returning with a depth that only maturity and understanding could bring.

And what about her? Had her feelings changed completely? Again, a few weeks ago he'd have said, of course. She was marrying someone else, someone she professed to be in love with. But that was before he'd seen the utter devastation in her face when she'd learned of a ten-year-old deception.

Maybe she did have feelings for him, something beyond the desire her kiss had communicated. The implications were a little scary. The idea that she'd carried some sort of torch for him all these years, even as she looked down her nose at him and treated him with utter disdain, colored the way he saw her, their history—everything. It also fueled his hope that his plans for the future weren't just a pipe dream.

IT WAS AFTER MIDNIGHT when Sonya arrived home. McPhee—or rather John-Michael, as she was determined to call him from now on—carried their bags into the foyer, then went to garage her car.

Matilda was still up when Sonya went into the kitchen to grab herself a glass of milk, and maybe a couple of cookies, before bed. All that glaring honesty on the trip home had made her hungry.

"Sorry, no chocolate chip," Matilda said. "Dr. Cason nixed them. Now we have to make do with low-fat oatmeal raisin." And the milk was skim. Blech.

Sonya drank the milk and ate the cookies, anyway. She hadn't exactly been the queen of healthy eating the last couple of days.

"Your mother wanted to see you when you got home," Matilda said.

"Now? It's late. Anyway, I talked to her just a few hours ago." She'd called her mother frequently over the past two days, just to make sure everything was okay. Muffy had assured her she was fine.

"I know. She wants you to wake her up. She has something she wants to show you."

Sonya was sure it could wait, but she dutifully trooped up to her mother's suite and tapped on the door. When she got no answer, she eased the door open. The bedside light was on, but Muffy had fallen asleep reading the newspaper.

She hoped Matilda or June had removed the sections that featured stories about war, politics and global warming, leaving only the light features.

Sonya gently removed her mother's half-moon reading glasses. Muffy stirred. "Oh, Sonya, honey, you're home."

"I didn't mean to wake you. Why don't you go back to sleep? We can talk in the morning."

Muffy pushed herself up. "I know you're probably tired, but I just want to show you this one thing." She shuffled through the various sections of the paper, finally settling on *Houston Living,* which came as an insert in the Houston paper.

"Judy Crandall's daughter got married last weekend, and look at the spread she got on her wedding. You'd think she was a princess or something."

"Yes, it's very nice," Sonya said noncommittally.

"This rag has been talking about her wedding for months, building everybody up to a fever pitch. Then, look, she actually had live doves in her wedding cake. When she cut the cake, the doves flew out like some miraculous thing. Can you imagine how dramatic that must have been?"

"Mother, you aren't suggesting I have live doves in *my* cake, are you? Mr. Phillips at the country club would have a fit. They'd probably fly around in a panic, pooping on the hors d'oeuvres—"

"All right, maybe not doves. But we've got to do something even better. What about butterflies? Can't you just see a cloud of exotic butterflies fluttering out of your cake—"

"They're bugs, Mother. Insects. No way."

"What if we did rose petals, then? A giant net, suspended above the dance floor. And when you and Marvin are dancing the waltz, a gentle shower of red and white rose petals could sprinkle over you. And they could continue to fall throughout the evening until the floor is covered with a carpet of fragrant petals…"

"Maybe," Sonya said. She could live with rose petals. Then she remembered that it would never happen, and she felt another pang of guilt. "Did you say the waltz?"

"Of course, dear. You know how to waltz, right?"

"Um, yeah, sure." Not one step. Her mother had signed her up for ballroom dancing when she was twelve, but she'd skipped out of almost every class as soon as Mrs. Linghorn had taken attendance. In cotillion, she'd sneaked out the back and smoked cigarettes with the cool kids rather than let some sweaty teenage boy drape his arms around her. At her debut, she'd placed her dainty white pumps on her escort's feet and let him move her around the dance floor. But it didn't matter. She didn't need to learn how to waltz because the reception wasn't going to happen.

"I'll arrange for you to take a refresher course on the waltz," Muffy said. "And some other dances, as well. It wouldn't hurt for you and Marvin to learn to foxtrot and tango. I don't want you tripping all over yourselves when everyone's watching."

"I'll set up the lessons," Sonya said dutifully. "You tell me who to call. You're supposed to let me do the legwork, remember?"

"Right. And the rose petals? You'll look into it?"

"Yes, Mother. Now go to sleep."

"The flight home was all right?" Muffy asked as Sonya cleared the newspapers away.

"It was—" She stopped, her eyes riveted on a headline relegated to the very last page of *Houston Living*. "Um, it was fine. No problems. Good night, Mother." She kissed Muffy on the cheek and retreated, the magazine tucked under her arm.

In the hallway she read the story more carefully. It was only about four inches of type, so it didn't take long. The headline read Out of Town Bride. The byline was Leslie Frazier's, the perky redheaded reporter who had accosted Sonya outside the hospital.

The gist of the story was that Leslie had been trying to get an interview with "society bride Sonya Patterson," but that elusive Sonya had repeatedly refused to be interviewed or had been out of town. Leslie speculated how an absentee bride could possibly plan a wedding with a gravely ill mother and a fiancé who was Missing in Action.

It was only a matter of time before Muffy got wind of this, Sonya thought in a panic. Muffy hated negative press. Sonya would have to nip this in the bud. She remembered deleting a few messages from the persistent reporter that had come through on her private line here at the house. Perhaps tomorrow she'd better call Ms. Frazier and wax enthusiastic over her upcoming nuptials, or the nosy reporter might get too curious and uncover much more than Sonya wanted to reveal.

JOHN-MICHAEL HADN'T LIKED Leslie Frazier the first time he'd encountered her, in front of the hospital trying to dig up dirt on Muffy. She called herself a reporter, but she was more of a gossipmonger, more interested in juicy tidbits than balanced journalism.

He liked her less after listening to the conversation between her and Sonya for the past forty-five minutes. He should have just stayed out in the car. But duty, not to mention a cold front, had propelled him to walk Sonya inside the newspaper building and all the way to Leslie Frazier's office.

Sonya had dressed for the occasion in a creamy white wool dress with berry-colored trim that reminded John-Michael of raspberry-swirl ice cream. Berry-colored, high-heeled ankle boots, matching purse, matching jacket—all contributed to her high-fashion image. It was the sort of outfit one saw on a runway, but few real women could pull it off.

Sonya carried with her a huge portfolio stuffed full of pictures and notes about the wedding.

John-Michael sat in a small lounge area just outside the door to Leslie's office. He'd brought a book to read while he waited—he never went anywhere without a book, because in the course of his job he did a lot of waiting around. But Leslie left the door to her office open, so he heard most of the conversation despite his best efforts not to listen.

Currently, the two women were discussing Sonya's gown. A Paris designer had created it for her, and a Houston seamstress would handle all the final fittings.

"I just purchased ten yards of Belgian lace for the edge of the train, and also here and here," Sonya enthused, sounding for all the world like the bubble-headed bride he'd thought her to be not long ago. "Monsieur LeBreque allowed for some flexibility so my mother and I could incorporate personal preferences within the framework of textile choices he recommended."

"Speaking of your mother," Leslie said, "what's her condition?"

"Oh, she's ecstatic about the wedding. She's having the time of her life helping me plan, and honestly I couldn't do it without her."

"I meant her physical condition. Tootsie Milford confirmed that Mrs. Patterson is in cardiac rehab. Was there a cardiac event?"

"She went in for some tests," Sonya said firmly. "Her doctor has recommended a cardiac-health regimen to prevent problems in the future."

It wasn't exactly a lie, John-Michael mused. June, the secretary, had crafted a cleverly worded statement, from which Sonya was quoting. Muffy did *not* want the press speculating that she was dying.

"Now, would you like to see a picture of the cake?" Sonya asked brightly, though her voice had a brittle edge. "The entire thing is edible—even these sculpted doves. And each layer offers a unique dietary experience. We have a sugar-free layer for diabetics, a low-carb layer for the Atkins folks, an angel-food layer for the Weight-Watchers crowd, a whole-wheat layer sweetened with honey, topped with tofu icing for the health-food types."

John-Michael rolled his eyes. He'd never heard of such a gimmicky wedding cake.

"It must be a very tall cake," Leslie said.

"Almost six feet."

"My goodness! That's almost taller than the groom! What does Marvin have to say about all this?" Leslie's tone was deceptively casual, and John-Michael went on alert. She suspected something was up. No one had seen Marvin in weeks, and a few of Sonya's friends had become openly curious.

"You know men," Sonya said in a conspiratorial tone. "He has no interest in the details of the wedding. He's ecstatic with whatever I decide."

"What about showers? Are you planning any?"

"Oh, sure! My maid of honor, Cissy Trask-Burnside, is planning a couples shower for December. Since it's winter, she's doing a tropical theme, and she's rented out the Houston Aquarium for the event."

John-Michael wondered if Sonya was going to come clean before that stomach-turning party. How would she explain Marvin's absence at his own shower? And how could she, in good conscience, allow Cissy to spend all that money on a shower for a nonexistent wedding, or accept gifts she knew she would have to return?

This morning he'd tried to talk Sonya into telling Muffy the truth. There was no need for her to announce to the world at large that she'd been victimized by a con man, he'd reasoned. She could simply say that she and Marvin had changed their minds about getting married. But the longer Sonya put off her confession, the harder it would be on Muffy when she finally learned the unpleasant story.

"One more week," Sonya had promised. "She has an

appointment with Dr. Cason next Monday. After he examines her, I'll ask him if she's well enough to withstand a shock. If he says yes, I'll tell her. If not, we'll have to keep up the pretext a while longer."

John-Michael would never do anything to endanger Muffy's health. He would go with what the cardiologist recommended. But the minute Dr. Cason said Muffy was strong enough, John-Michael intended to hold Sonya to her word.

Meanwhile, being forced to listen to all these froufrou wedding plans was about to make him heave.

"I have the menu here," Sonya said in response to Leslie's question about food at the reception. "The Thousand Acres Country Club has one of the best chefs in Houston, as I'm sure you know, so Mother and I were only too happy to let him guide us in our menu selections. We'll be starting with a lobster bisque…"

The way Sonya was talking, the wedding sounded very, very real. He wondered how many hours Sonya had spent fantasizing about being the Princess Bride, the center of everyone's attention, wonder and envy, and how much it bothered her that this extravaganza would never take place.

She was putting on a show for her mother's sake. But how much of it was for Sonya's sake? Was she delaying the inevitable return to Earth because she wanted to extend the fantasy for herself, bask in the attention just a bit longer?

"The Brent Warren Orchestra will be playing a handselected list of classic, romantic torch songs and dance music mixed with some newer songs," Sonya answered when Leslie asked about the reception music. "And we're cooking up a special treat—I don't want to give too much away, but it's something I hope everyone will remember."

"You're not doing a wedding cake full of doves, are you?" Leslie asked dryly.

"Oh, no, no. Nothing that involves…creatures."

John-Michael could almost see Sonya shiver with revulsion, and it made him smile. She used to be such a little tomboy, but some time after the age of twelve she'd developed a healthy distrust of critters. Cats, dogs and horses were okay. Parrots were tolerable but even doves were highly suspect. On the other side of the spectrum, rodents were completely disgusting, and she was terrified of anything with more than four legs. She refused to go outside if there was any chance she might encounter flying grasshoppers, cicadas or clingy june bugs.

She was such a complete girlie-girl, which was why he found the idea of her pursuing a career in engineering so hard to swallow. But he supposed those two weren't incompatible, just not something the world was used to seeing—an engineer who jumped on a chair when she saw a spider.

She'd started work on her résumé that morning.

They wound up the hour-long interview with talk about reception gifts. Every female guest would receive a Limoges box, whatever that was, and the males would receive a deck of brass playing cards. John-Michael couldn't imagine anything he needed less. But then, he probably wouldn't have been invited to the wedding even if it did take place. As of January 8, he was no longer Sonya's bodyguard.

Usually that thought cheered him up, but today it seemed a little depressing. He knew he would worry about her. He wondered if Muffy would hire someone to replace him once she learned the wedding was off. Then he felt an immediate, irrational stab of jealousy that someone else would spend twenty-four hours a day with his Sonya.

His Sonya. Now that was an odd way to think about it.

The women wound up their conversation and emerged from the office. John-Michael hastily opened his book, pretending to have been absorbed in it the whole time. He looked up.

"Done already?" he asked innocently.

The reporter stepped in front of Sonya, all feline grace and kittenish smile. "I don't believe we've been formally introduced. Leslie Frazier."

"John-Michael McPhee," he said, taking the hand she offered. She held his just a bit too long.

"So you're Sonya's bodyguard?"

"Yes, ma'am."

"I saw you at the hospital and I wondered. You're even better looking in person than they said."

Behind her, Sonya rolled her eyes and made gagging gestures. John-Michael stifled a grin. "Thank you." He didn't know what else to say.

"You take care of our little Sonya, now," she said, exaggerating her southern drawl. "While Marvin's away," she added, as if she knew a secret.

"Oh, Sonya, that reminds me," John-Michael said. "Marvin called on my cell while you were in your meeting. He said you must have had your phone turned off."

"Oh," Sonya said, looking pained, "you should have interrupted me."

"I was going to, but he said I shouldn't. He just wanted to tell you that he'd found a store in Hong Kong that sold your grandmother's silver pattern, and he wanted to know if he should buy the pieces to replace the ones that were missing." The fabrication had just jumped into John-Michael's mind, but he thought it sounded plausible.

"Oh, yes, I would love to have the set finished out!" Sonya said passionately. She turned to Leslie. "The pattern is impossible to find anymore," she explained. Then she focused again on John-Michael. "What did you tell him?"

"I told him I thought you would want him to buy any he could find, and he said he thought that, too."

"Oh, good."

"And he'll call you later. It's very early in the morning in Hong Kong. He'd just gotten up, and he wanted to catch you before he got stalled all day in meetings."

Sonya's mouth spread into a sickly sweet smile. "Oh, he's so thoughtful."

She didn't say anything else until they were sitting in her BMW, far away from prying ears. "Thank you for what you did back there. Leslie is definitely getting suspicious, but I think our little act convinced her."

"You're welcome. I think."

"Where in the world did you come up with that story about Grandmother's silver?"

He tapped his mystery novel on his knee. "I got it from this book. The hero is a butler, and his employer is trying to finish out an antique silver pattern that was her grandmother's."

"You lie very convincingly."

"So do you, I might point out. With that act you did for Leslie, you had *me* convinced the wedding was really going to happen. And that you were on cloud nine about it."

Sonya tipped her head back against the headrest and closed her eyes. "It was one of the most exhausting conversations I've ever had. I wonder how Marvin does it, maintaining a charade for day after day, week after week? I did it for an hour and I feel like I need a blood transfusion."

"You mean you weren't having fun?"

"Fun? Pretending I was happy about a wedding to a complete jerk?"

"Don't most little girls like to pretend?"

"Very funny." She still hadn't started the car. Driving her own BMW—her fourth since the one she got for high school graduation—had been her idea. She'd decided she needed more driving experience. "Maybe I should let you drive home."

"Oh, no. Another six weeks and I won't be around. You'll have to drive to job interviews, maybe to and from work. You need the practice."

"Meaning, only a spoiled brat can afford to drive just when she feels like it. Okay. But it's rush hour out there." Houston's rush hour was any time after three o'clock.

AFTER THIRTY MINUTES on I-110, during which they'd gone half a mile, Sonya couldn't take it anymore. She took the next exit.

"Where are we going?" John-Michael asked.

"To a bar. I need a drink."

"I'll take a taxi home, thanks."

"A coffee bar, of course. I'm a bad enough driver sober."

"But what about the kids? Don't you have to pick them up from day care? And won't your husband want dinner on the table when he gets home?"

Sonya groaned. "I honestly don't know how some women do it. Are you trying to *prove* I'm spoiled?"

"Just trying to prepare you for life in the real world, if that's what you're determined to live."

"Perhaps I'll take the bus to work. I can read metallurgy reports and do stress calculations while I commute."

John-Michael snorted.

"Oh, so now you're laughing at the idea of me riding a bus?"

"Have you ever ridden a bus?"

"No. But how hard could it be?"

"Ask me that again after you've tried it."

She pulled into a Starbucks. She hadn't had a toffee nut latte in days. She got out of the car, strode inside the coffee shop and up to the counter. After she'd placed her order, she turned to John-Michael. "What do you want? My treat."

"Oh." He looked startled. "Just a regular coffee."

She realized she probably hadn't ever bought him coffee before. She usually sent him in to buy whatever she wanted and didn't bother with the money, either. Muffy provided all the employees with plenty of cash for incidentals. But traveling around with Brenna and Cindy, she'd gotten used to being the one in charge, particularly when she was the only one with a means to pay.

When they called her name, she went up to the counter and picked up both of their beverages, handing his coffee to him. "There you are, John-Michael." It was the first time she'd called him by his given name, at least to his face, in over a decade. It felt very strange.

Judging from the look on John-Michael's face, it sounded strange, too.

He nodded and hoisted his paper cup in a toast. "To…to your new future. Whatever it may hold."

Sonya lifted her cup, too. "And yours." She had this sudden, silly picture in her mind of her and John-Michael entwining their arms before sipping from their coffees. Must be all the wedding talk.

Chapter Seven

John-Michael had been dreading this appointment with the seamstress. The Belgian lace had arrived, and Mrs. Kim wanted Sonya to try on the dress so she could experiment using the lace in different ways. John-Michael didn't know how many ways there were to use lace, but he was guessing quite a few, which meant another tedious wait.

He'd brought two books with him this time.

Mrs. Kim had a tony shop in River Oaks, where she specialized in custom-tailoring wedding dresses, bridesmaid dresses, debutante ball gowns, and anything else Houston's high-society females could come up with. According to Muffy, anyone who was anybody had her wedding dress nipped and tucked by Mrs. Kim.

John-Michael sat in the shop's main area, decorated with huge color photographs of society wedding dresses Mrs. Kim had presumably sewn or tailored. The shop was decorated in shades of pink, lavender and mauve, with tiny French-Provincial-style chairs and crystal bowls filled with potpourri littering every surface.

John-Michael felt like the proverbial bull in a china shop as he perched uneasily on one of the delicate chairs, once again relegated to involuntary eavesdropping.

"You been losing weight," Mrs. Kim scolded from inside the airplane-hangar-sized dressing room. "Every bride the same. She either stuff herself with cake for six months and swell up like the Goodyear blimp, or she stop eating altogether and turn into a skeleton."

"I eat plenty," Sonya said amid the swish of silk and lace, the whisper of chiffon. "It must be my mother's new heart-healthy menu and exercise regimen. I've been doing it with her."

John-Michael tried to banish from his mind the image of Sonya, wearing perhaps a virginal white thong and demibra, slithering into the frothy concoction she'd once planned to wear for her wedding. What would happen to this dress, so lovingly designed, meticulously constructed, using the finest textiles? After all her hard work, would Mrs. Kim be disappointed when there were no bridal pictures to put on her wall, no mention of her handiwork in the newspaper write-up?

The wanton spending of cash for no good reason bothered John-Michael to no end. Sonya had reasoned that Muffy would never really miss the money—she had more than enough to squander some occasionally. She was contributing to the local economy, providing work to people like Mrs. Kim. As for the florist and musicians, they would pocket the hefty deposits and not mind a bit. But after a lifetime spent carefully budgeting his money and his father's, he hated witnessing careless waste.

"Oh, you make such a beautiful bride," Mrs. Kim said with genuine-sounding awe in her voice.

John-Michael wanted to see.

"Turn around, dear, so you can see the back in the mirror."

"Oh, it really is lovely," Sonya said, a catch in her voice. Maybe she was mourning the fact that absolutely no one but Mrs. Kim would ever see her wearing the lace confection. Of course, she could keep the dress until she found someone else to marry. But maybe that was considered tacky, getting married in a dress you selected for a wedding to some other groom.

"Now, we can gather the lace full like this, or have it more relaxed, like this," Mrs. Kim explained.

"I like the more relaxed look," Sonya said wistfully. "I promised my mother I would take pictures and get her opinion, though. I brought my digital camera. It's in that bag over there."

"I can't take picture and hold the lace in place at the same time," Mrs. Kim said.

"Oh. Well, maybe John-Michael wouldn't mind. John-Michael?"

"Yes? I'm sorry, did you call me?" he asked, as if he hadn't been hanging on every word of conversation.

"Yes. Could you come in here and take a couple of pictures for my mother?"

"Isn't it bad luck to be seen in your wedding dress before the ceremony?"

"Only if you're the groom," she said impatiently.

Oh. Right.

"I know it's beyond the scope of your duties," she

said, "but would you please? Mrs. Kim's hands are going to cramp up."

He was already out of his chair. "I'm coming." And he entered Mrs. Kim's inner sanctum.

The sight of Sonya all in ivory satin, standing on a pedestal like one of those spinning ballerinas in a little girl's music box, nearly knocked John-Michael off his feet. He'd always known Sonya was uncommonly beautiful, even for a privileged woman with all the most expensive beauty treatments at her disposal. But in that wedding dress she looked truly regal, a bride fit for a prince.

He felt this strange twinge around his heart, and for a few stupid seconds he yearned to be the prince who claimed her as his own. The sight of her actually made him light-headed.

"John-Michael?" Sonya said, her voice coming to him out of a thick fog.

"You look so beautiful." The words slipped out involuntarily, causing Mrs. Kim to beam and Sonya to blush furiously.

"She going to be my prettiest bride ever," Mrs. Kim said proudly.

"Th-the camera's in my bag over there," Sonya stammered, nodding toward her tote bag.

John-Michael managed to tear his gaze away from Sonya long enough to find the tote bag, find the camera, remove it from its case. He'd used it before. Sonya often asked him to be her photographer, chronicling important moments in her life. He recalled, though, that he'd never taken any pictures of her and Marvin—

Marvin had always weaseled out of it. That was one of the things that had alerted John-Michael to the possibility that Marvin was up to no good.

"Here's choice number one," Mrs. Kim said, gathering the lace tightly and holding it against the edge of the voluminous train. John-Michael dutifully snapped a couple of pictures. "Now, here is choice number two." He didn't see much difference, but snapped away.

"Take a few pictures of Sonya without me in the frame," Mrs. Kim said. "Mrs. Patterson has not yet seen her daughter wearing the dress."

John-Michael snapped a few more, his heart aching. Beauty had never made him hurt before. Maybe it was the fact this particular beauty was so unattainable that caused his pain. In that moment he wanted her worse than he'd ever wanted anyone in his life.

Timing was everything, he kept telling himself.

Watching her prepare for this wedding had made this week one of the more uncomfortable of John-Michael's life. No matter how many times he told himself it wasn't real, it was never going to happen, he still knew deep down that if Marvin hadn't turned out to be a crook, it *would* be happening for real. He would be losing her forever. Even Marvin's betrayal only delayed the inevitable. Someday she would find someone else, and today's fiction would become tomorrow's fact. That realization only made him more determined to investigate the potential between them, before he lost her again.

He checked his shots in the viewfinder to be sure they'd turned out all right. "That should do it, I think," he said. "Anything else, Miss Patterson?" Sometimes, just to get her goat, he played up their mistress-servant relationship in front of other people. Or maybe as a reminder to himself that he had a long row to hoe.

"No, thank you," she said, not even bothering to try to covertly get back at him, the way she usually did. Now he felt guilty for needling her. She'd done nothing to deserve it except look lovely.

He returned to his book, which had lost its appeal, and waited for Sonya to reappear in her street clothes. She'd dressed down today in a gold turtleneck, black wool blazer, slim black pants and flat-heeled boots. He could almost see her in a professional environment when she dressed like that. But her hair was done up the way she'd planned to wear it for the wedding, tortured into an elaborate maze of twists, curls and braids.

He remembered when she used to wear it long and loose, how it used to look after she went for a swim, then combed it out and let it dry in the sun, which provided the natural blond highlights she now paid more than a hundred dollars a month to artificially reproduce.

"Ready," she said as she emerged. He covertly checked her over, to reassure himself that she was once again an ordinary woman, rather than a goddess. But he had to admit that some part of her goddesslike persona clung to her even dressed in black. Or maybe it had always been there.

"Will you keep the dress?" he asked when they were once again alone in her car.

"I was thinking I might donate it to charity. There's

a foundation that sells donated wedding dresses to fund dreams for breast-cancer patients."

"And when you get married again, you'll just have another one made?"

She gave him a look he could only describe as sober. "I'm never doing this again. I never realized how silly it all is. A big, silly party to impress our supposed friends. The important thing isn't the wedding with all the ridiculous trimmings, it's the vows. And the life that comes after, of course. It could be accomplished just as easily at a little chapel, with the people you care most about there as witnesses. And all the money that's spent on flowers and lobster bisque could be used to fund scholarships or buy books for underfunded libraries—or give the couple a start on life. For what Muffy is paying for this wedding, I could make a down payment on a house."

"And what made you come to this noble conclusion?"

"After you take away the vows and the marriage— which I've had to do—you see what's left. And without all the trite, romantic rationale brides use to wallow in their excesses, it's easier to see that what's left is essentially meaningless."

"It's an important rite of passage," John-Michael argued.

"Yes. And I don't mean to downplay the importance. I'm not against weddings per se. But a party and a white dress shouldn't be the highlight of a woman's life."

"So you don't plan to get married?"

"Oh, I imagine I'll get married someday. But you can

be damn sure it won't be anything like this. I can't wait until next Monday. I'll explain the whole thing to Dr. Cason, and I'm sure he'll give me medical clearance to tell Mother the truth."

When she looked again at John-Michael, she had tears in her eyes. "I really can't keep up this pretense much longer. It's so hard to pretend I'm happy."

"Pull over," he said. And she did, finding a spot in a parking lot. She found a monogrammed handkerchief in her purse and dabbed at her eyes, trying not to smear her makeup.

"I'm sorry. It seems all I've done lately is snivel."

"You're allowed. It's an emotional time."

"I wish now I had just told Mother the truth when Marvin first went missing. You were right. It's just going to be worse now."

"I was right? Hold it, let me find my calendar and circle this day in red. Sonya said I was right."

She reached out and thumped him on the arm. "Cut it out, McPhee." But she was smiling, he noticed, through the tears. "I mean, John-Michael. I don't know if you noticed, but I *have* been trying not to be so horrible to you."

"I've noticed. And I'm still teasing you. I'll try to be better."

"That's okay. I like your teasing, most of the time. You know, when you're in junior high, if a boy teases you, it's a sure sign he has a crush on you."

He did have a crush on her, and he was on the verge of telling her so. But then he remembered the incredible stress she was under and decided to hold his tongue. Just a while longer.

"You want me to drive?" he asked, hoping she was enough absorbed in her own misery not to notice his yearning.

"No, I think I've pulled myself together sufficiently to get us home in one piece. I'm doing better on the freeways, huh?"

"You're doing great," he said, because he genuinely wanted her to feel good about something. Was that the definition of love? When you did things to make another person happy, with no expectation of getting something in return?

He hadn't felt that way about Sonya since she was ten, and he'd turned himself inside out for nothing more than the pleasure of her smile—before desire and need, duty and responsibility had complicated their relationship.

LESLIE FRAZIER'S ARTICLE came out in the following Sunday's *Houston Living* insert. Muffy had the story spread out over the dining room, reading every word aloud between bites of her whole-wheat pancakes and sips of green tea. She looked a hundred percent better than she had even a week ago, stylishly decked out in her teal warm-up suit, ready for her session with her personal trainer.

Sonya wore her workout clothes, too. She was participating in her mother's workouts to show her support and make it more fun for Muffy, but Sonya was benefiting, too. She needed some way to relieve the stress of planning a nonwedding and the constant presence of John-Michael McPhee. Just the sight of him created a pleasure-pain connection in her brain, now. Pleasure because he was so nice to look at. Pain because she knew damn well she couldn't have him. She should have made something of her life years ago, back when she first acknowledged her desire for him. Because John-Michael wasn't going to waste his attentions on a woman without substance, no matter how well-groomed.

Maybe someday she would have substance. By then, though, it would be too late. John-Michael would be gone, married to another cop or an E.R. nurse or an assistant district attorney, someone hardworking and intelligent he met through work. Someone he'd never had the opportunity to meet while tied to Sonya.

"Sonya, you're not even listening."

"Sorry, Mother."

"I was just wondering if Ms. Frazier asked who was giving you away."

That was a bit of a sore subject. Since Sonya's father was deceased, and she had no living male relatives other than a couple of great uncles she'd never met, she hadn't been able to think of who should give her away, and had decided Muffy should do the honors.

Muffy had declared that was too untraditional.

"The subject came up. But I was thinking—now, this would be a bit strange, but what if I asked Jock McPhee to give me away?"

Muffy's eyebrows arched so high they disappeared into her red-gold hair, but she also wore the ghost of a smile. "You want the gardener to give you away?"

"He's more than that. He's really the only father figure I've ever known. He was so kind to me after Daddy died. And, yes, people would talk, but so what? A wedding should be about true feelings, not trying to impress people."

Muffy unexpectedly got a little misty-eyed over that sentiment. "Well, it's your wedding. And I wouldn't mind seeing what Jock McPhee would look like with a clean shave and a tux."

"He's a handsome man," Sonya said.

"Yes, he is," Muffy said softly.

Sonya was surprised Muffy had given in so easily. She'd floated the idea mostly to see how her mother would react. Having so recently seen herself in an unattractive light, and having vowed to change, she wanted to see whether her mother might be open to seeing things in a different light, too.

Apparently she was.

"Do you think he'd be willing to do it?" Sonya asked.

"Oh, I think so. You know, he brought me the most beautiful flowers in the hospital."

"He can be so kind. Oh, that reminds me. He's going to make my bridal bouquet from our own hothouse roses."

"He'll do a lovely job." Muffy threatened to mist up again, so she distracted herself with shuffling through the paper. "Oh, my goodness, look at this. They still haven't caught that horrible man who caused all the trouble at the International Jewelry Consortium show in New York a few weeks ago."

Sonya's heart jumped into her throat. "You heard about that?"

"Everyone heard about it! I was still in the hospital, but Tootsie filled me in. She said a woman went berserk, climbed up over the buffet table and broke the arm off an ice sculpture."

"Oh, my gosh." Panicked, Sonya whipped the paper out of her mother's hands and scanned the article. The woman in question, of course, was Brenna. Her ungainly leap into a pile of shrimp was part of the same chase that had culminated in Marvin plunging down an elevator shaft.

There was still no mention of Marvin's real name, thank God. She relaxed. "I know this woman," Sonya said, amused all over again by the story. "I met her in Dallas when I was there." Her mother still thought she'd spent most of her time out of town at a health spa in Dallas. "Her father owns the Thompson-Lanier store."

"Oh, that Thompson. Well, I'm sure her father must be mortified over this debacle."

Actually, Marcus Thompson had been rather proud that Brenna had tried her best to catch the crook who'd stolen from her and her parents. But Sonya didn't want to draw any more attention to the incident in New York. Tomorrow, after her mother's appointment with Dr. Cason, she would hopefully be able to tell Muffy everything. Then it would be time to start preparing for their trip to Boston. She was determined to join the others if she possibly could.

"There's the doorbell," Sonya said with relief. "That must be Butch." Butch was her mother's new trainer, a handsome bundle of muscles who was gently introducing Muffy to the concepts of strength training and aerobics. Today they were going for a walk around the neighborhood. Sonya folded up the newspaper and covertly stuffed it in a trash basket on their way to greet Butch.

IN ANOTHER PART OF HOUSTON, a dark-haired man smoked a Cuban cigar and leafed through the Sunday paper as a busty masseuse gave his back muscles a workout.

After the debacle in New York, when he'd come closer to getting caught than ever before, he'd decided to lay low for a while. He'd dyed his hair brown, grown a goatee, and he'd switched to wearing his contact lenses. Back here in Houston, he was just another anonymous businessman in a luxury hotel.

He started to toss the *Houston Living* magazine aside, but then he was inexorably drawn to it. The magazine detailed the lives of the city's rich and richer, the same people he had hobnobbed with during his brief engagement to Sonya Patterson. He wondered what Sonya was up to, how she'd recovered from being jilted.

He didn't kid himself that she'd really suffered much. He'd cleaned her out of her ready cash, jewelry and furs, but that wasn't much when compared to the vast Patterson fortune she had access to. She had no doubt ducked under her mother's protective wing, cried a few tears, than gone about her life.

He'd actually had the idea that he might marry Sonya. It was a cinch he wasn't going to inherit any of his own family money. His parents had pretty much disowned him. With Sonya being the only heir to her father's oil company, he'd have been set for life. He could have worked or not, as he pleased, lived any place he wanted, driven any kind of fancy sports car that caught his eye.

He'd even thought he might be in love with Sonya. She was beautiful, lively, intelligent—a fitting partner, someone even his parents would approve of. But he'd started to worry about that bodyguard of hers. And he'd also realized that Sonya didn't have ready access to the bulk of the Patterson millions, which meant neither would he. He'd gently queried Muffy Patterson about allowing him to serve as her financial manager, but she'd sweetly refused him, saying once he'd been in the family a few years and better understood their philosophy of life, she might consider letting him play a role in the handling of the fortune that would one day be his and Sonya's.

He hadn't wanted to wait. His feet had been itchy. So when the opportunity arose, he'd taken all that was available—over a hundred-thousand-dollars' worth—and took off.

After all that had happened lately, he wondered if he'd made the right decision. Better a dull life as Sonya's kept man, with an allowance, than a four-by-six jail cell. But the threat of jail was fading. The authorities were no closer to catching him than they'd ever been. He wasn't sure they even knew his true identity. Unfortunately, he'd lost much of what he'd stolen—the Picasso, most of the jewelry and a good bit of cash, all recovered by authorities. He needed another score, another woman.

He flipped through the magazine's pages, recognizing a few faces. Then he stopped cold. There was Sonya, smiling broadly from the page. And there he was, right beside her. It was their engagement portrait. The headline on the four-page spread was Dream Winter Wedding.

The masseuse picked that moment to dig deep into Marvin's deltoids, and he yelped in pain.

"Oops, sorry. Was that too hard?"

She didn't sound sorry, but he decided to let it pass. "You can go now. I'm done."

"Your hour isn't up yet."

"That's okay. Run along."

When he was dressed, he retreated to his room to read the article carefully. Sonya had not called off the wedding. Why? Was it possible she didn't even know she'd been jilted? He'd given her a cover story about being in Hong Kong and then Beijing for the next few weeks on an important business trip, to delay her discovering he'd stolen from her. But maybe, by the time she'd noticed all the money missing from her account, she didn't associate it with his departure. Maybe she'd blamed it on an accounting error—or maybe she hadn't yet noticed it. She never balanced her checkbook that he could tell.

And the furs—they'd been stowed in an upstairs closet. It hadn't gotten terribly cold in Houston yet this winter. Maybe she hadn't even looked.

There was no way she could miss the jewelry theft, but she could have blamed it on someone else, like that reprobate gardener.

He read the article again. It sure sounded like she was still devoted to him.

He pondered the problem all that day and into the next, finally deciding there would be no harm in at least talking to Sonya on his new, throw-away cell phone. It was possible the authorities hadn't yet connected his real name to his various criminal activities. If so, there was still a way to salvage the situation.

He could still marry Sonya. He might have to wait a few years, but he could still have all that delicious money.

Chapter Eight

"You are doing incredibly well, Mrs. Patterson," Dr. Cason said with a warm smile. Sonya and Muffy were sitting in his well-appointed office in the medical building next to the hospital, going over Muffy's most recent test results.

"I've been doing everything you recommended," Muffy said proudly. "I'm walking and swimming and doing strength training, I have a nice Indian man named Mihir who is teaching me yoga and meditation. And my diet—I haven't had even one bite of cheesecake. My cook has risen to the challenge, and she's been serving me the most delicious meals. I'm even starting to like oatmeal."

Dr. Cason's smile grew wider. "That's wonderful. Nothing makes me happier than seeing a patient change her life for the better. With that attitude, you'll live to be a hundred."

"Is there anything we should be careful of?" Sonya asked. "For example—would it be okay if my mother watched a very scary movie? Something with…shocking moments?"

"Sonya," Muffy objected, "you know I can't stand to watch scary movies."

"I was just using that as an example."

"There's no immediate danger of a recurring thrombosis," Dr. Cason said. "The heart muscle suffered no permanent damage, and it's functioning very well. The surgery I did eliminated the arterial clogging. The main focus now should be to prevent the dangerous plaque from building up again."

"So she's strong enough to withstand an emotional upset? If we should receive tragic news—like a death in the family. We don't need to protect her?"

"Sonya, has someone died?" Muffy asked, sounding alarmed.

"No, no, Mother." Sonya laid a hand on Muffy's arm. "I'm just talking theoretically."

"You need to be more concerned about long-term outlook," Dr. Cason said. "An emotional upset, while not pleasant, isn't likely to do harm to your mother's health unless her reaction is prolonged and turns into depression or chronic anxiety."

Well, that pretty much told Sonya what she needed to know. She could not put off telling Muffy about Marvin's betrayal any longer. She would do it during dinner tonight, she decided. And she would ask John-Michael to join them, for moral support. Just in case she wanted to chicken out at the last minute.

"Dr. Cason," Muffy asked, sounding uncharacteristically tentative, "is it all right for me to resume, uh, romantic relations?"

What? Sonya stared at her mother, who wouldn't

meet her gaze. Why would Muffy ask that? She wasn't involved with anyone. She hadn't even dated since Sonya's father had died, proclaiming loudly to anyone who asked that there was only one man for her in this lifetime.

"As long as you're not participating in the sexual Olympics," Dr. Cason said with a little laugh, not embarrassed at all. He must be used to talking about such things with his patients, but Sonya was shocked to the core. "And no Viagra," he added.

Sonya waited until they were in the elevator to say anything. "Mother, do you have a boyfriend I don't know about?"

"No, dear," she said with a sly smile. "That question was strictly theoretical, just like yours."

"Oh. It's just that I can't imagine—"

"Why not? I'm still young. I'm reasonably attractive, I'm losing weight and getting fit. By summer, I'll look decent in a bathing suit."

"Mother, I'd be only too pleased if you found someone," Sonya said, which was not entirely the truth. She would be profoundly disturbed if her mother started dating or, heaven forbid, remarried. But only because she was so used to having Muffy to herself. "The notion just took me by surprise, that's all. Has Butch made a pass at you?" She would take the muscle-bound trainer apart sinew by sinew.

"Good heavens, no. He's a tad young for me." And she giggled.

Tim and John-Michael were waiting with the limo

in front of the medical building. Tim hurried to open the back door for them.

"Let's go to Tiffany and buy something to celebrate," Muffy said. "Sonya, darling, do you have time, or are there wedding plans to worry about?"

"No, I have time. But this weather…are you sure you want to be out in it? Anyway, I don't really need any more jewelry."

"Good heavens, who are you and what have you done with my daughter? No child of mine could possibly utter those words. You're just tired of all the pieces you have, that's why you don't wear anything but your engagement ring anymore."

Arguing with Muffy took too much energy, so Sonya nodded weakly. When they pulled up in front of the mall a few minutes later, John-Michael opened his door. "I'll do the honors, Tim," he said. Then he opened the back door so Muffy and Sonya could exit the limo.

Muffy charged ahead into the mall, but John-Michael touched Sonya's arm, indicating she should hang back. "What did Dr. Cason say?"

Sonya considered fibbing. But putting it off longer would only make it harder. "She's medically cleared for any emotional upset. I was planning to tell her tonight, at dinner."

"It'll be a relief," he said. "Like pulling a sore tooth."

"I've never had a sore tooth, much less pulled one," she said dryly. John-Michael opened the door for her, and she entered the dry, overheated mall, hoping her mother wouldn't get too extravagant.

"Mrs. Patterson!" the man behind the counter at Tiffany said as Muffy and Sonya entered.

"Good afternoon, Paul," Muffy said. "I need a new pair of earrings. Do you have any sapphires?"

Just then Sonya's cell phone rang. She stepped away from the counter to answer it. "Hello?"

"Sonya, darling. It's me."

Sonya grabbed onto the closest thing for support, which happened to be John-Michael's arm. "M-Marvin?"

John-Michael grew instantly alert. "Act like there's nothing wrong," he whispered.

Nothing wrong? How was she going to pull that off? But she remembered that Brenna had done it. Marvin had such a colossal ego, he thought the women in love with him believed he could do no wrong and were willing to overlook or forgive anything.

"Sonya, I've missed you so much," he said. "You wouldn't believe what's been going on. I've been stranded in Beijing for absolute weeks! My passport was stolen, then there was this very scary military thing going on. I was completely out of communication."

"Oh, Marvin, I've been so worried. Are you all right?"

John-Michael nodded encouragingly.

"I'm fine, now that I hear your voice."

"When are you coming home? I mean, here, to Houston?"

"I don't know. I have to jump through all these diplomatic hoops just to get out of this country. But I'm absolutely positive I'll be there for the wedding."

"The wedding. Well, of course. But not before?"

"I'll do my best."

John-Michael was gesturing urgently. "Tell him everything's on schedule," he whispered.

"The wedding plans are right on schedule," she said. "I never doubted you would be here. I know how crazy your business can get."

"Is there anything else happening?"

"My mother's been ill. But she's better now. She'll be so pleased you called.

"Please give her my love. Anything else?"

Like all of my money and jewelry missing? That's what he was fishing for—whether she had actually figured out who had wiped her out.

She had a sudden brainstorm. "You just wouldn't believe it—someone sneaked into my suite and stole all of my jewelry. Mother thinks it was the cleaning service she hired to do the carpets, but there was no way to prove it."

"Darling, that's awful!"

"Don't worry, I still have my engagement ring. I never take that off. Then, I've also had trouble with the bank. They had some kind of computer glitch that just wiped out my checking account. The accountants are still trying to figure out what happened."

John-Michael nodded enthusiastically and gave her a thumb's-up for her creative lying.

"Oh, darling, how are you coping?" Marvin said solicitously. Sonya simply could not understand how she ever fell for his slimy pseudo empathy. "It must be awful."

"I'm fine, now that I know everything's okay with you."

"I have to go, love," he said. "I'll call you the moment I know when I'm going to be home."

"I'll keep my cell phone on."

He disconnected, and Sonya was so limp with the release of tension she almost fell down. She realized she was still clutching John-Michael's jacket, and she slowly released it.

"That was brilliant," John-Michael said excitedly.

"Sonya," Muffy called. "What are you two whispering about over there? Come here and look at these earrings."

Sonya dutifully joined her mother at the glass counter, where she had four pairs of dazzling earrings spread out on a velvet cloth.

"Which do you like best?"

"The amethyst drops are pretty. And they're not so fancy you couldn't wear them for everyday."

Muffy smiled. "Paul, I'll take the sapphires for me, and the amethysts for Sonya."

"Oh, no, Mother, I don't need—"

"Nonsense. You've been a most devoted daughter during the last few weeks, and I want to show my gratitude. Speaking of gratitude, I gave you a little job to do on your trip to Milwaukee. Did you do it?" And she glanced covertly at John-Michael.

"As a matter of fact, I did," Sonya whispered, wondering how she would ever get up the nerve to confess she'd never gone to California. "But I had to special-order the gift, and it hasn't arrived yet."

"Well, what did you get?" Muffy whispered.

"You'll see." She'd added some of her own money, income from her trust, to buy the present she'd selected, but it would be worth it. Maybe she and John-Michael weren't destined to be together, but every time he used the wonderful gift, she hoped he would think about her.

Later that afternoon, John-Michael waited until Muffy was safely ensconced with Mihir, her Indian guru, in the parlor she'd decked out as her "meditation room," before seeking out Sonya. He asked her to meet him in the greenhouse, where there was no chance they would be overheard.

"What are we going to do now?" Sonya asked miserably. They ambled along the greenhouse's long aisles, surrounded by the warm, moist air and the smell of dirt and peat and fertilizer. It was a pleasant smell, recalling John-Michael's childhood when he used to hang out here, doing small jobs for his father and looking forward to the day when he would be a real gardener. At age seven, he'd had no greater ambition. It was only when his father realized his only son wanted to follow in his footsteps that he chased John-Michael out of the greenhouse and told him to think bigger, to reach for the stars, that he could become anything he wanted to be.

"Marvin must have found out somehow that the wedding is still on," Sonya said, pausing to sniff a rose bloom, "If I call it off now—"

"Maybe you shouldn't call it off," John-Michael said, reversing his earlier position. "If he thinks the wedding's still on, that he's gotten away with his crime, maybe he'll actually show up here again."

"That's exactly what I was thinking. This might be our last chance to catch him, before he retires to some Caribbean island and disappears forever."

"Exactly."

"I can't deceive my mother any longer."

"I agree. We'll have to bring her into our confidence. This plan can only proceed if she agrees to keep up the pretense that a wedding is going to take place. Surely Marvin will return to Houston before too long."

"I don't know if I can do it," she said, her voice full of anguish. "Pretending to be a blushing bride-to-be— you just can't imagine how painful it is. And how humiliating when everyone finds out what happened. Can you imagine the heyday Tootsie Milford will have? And that wretched Leslie Frazier?"

He felt for Sonya. He really did. He'd thought she was enjoying her role as a bride a little too much. After listening to her performance on the phone with Marvin, he realized what a skilled actress Sonya was. She wasn't enjoying herself. The stress of the pretense was wearing her down.

"The worst part has been deceiving Muffy, right?"

Sonya nodded.

"You'll feel better once you come clean with your mom. If she pulls the plug on the wedding plans, it'll all be over."

"And we'll never catch Marvin." She balled up her fist and pounded it on the long bench. Nearby plants shuddered.

"Here, now." John-Michael took her clenched fist

and coaxed it open. "You need to relax. All this stress is not good for you."

"I've never been much good at relaxing," she said. "I never had a hobby I could lose myself in. The closest thing I can think of is when I'm lost in some complex equation. But I haven't done any engineering work in a long time."

"I hardly think quantum mechanics is the way to relax." He found a gardening apron and handed it to her. "Put this on."

"Oh, come on."

"I'm serious. Gardening is a very soothing activity. Digging your hands in the warm earth, nurturing living things—it's good for the soul."

"How would you know?"

"I'm my father's son in some ways," he said.

"All right." She put the apron on over her pristine, pale-gold sweater and darker gold jeans. "What should I do?"

"I see some little chrysanthemum bushes that need transplanting. Here's a pot and a spade. That container over there contains potting soil. Fill the pot about halfway."

She followed his directions, though she held the pot and the dirt as far away from herself as possible.

"Now set the pot down, and dig a hole in the center."

"With my hands? Shouldn't I have gloves on?"

"Your hands will wash."

She made a few tentative pokes at the dirt. John-Michael came behind her, put his larger hands on her pale, delicate ones, and pressed her fingers deep into the dirt. "Like this." He could smell her hair and her light perfume, sweeter and softer than anything growing in the greenhouse. He immediately grew hard, and he had to stop himself from deliberately stepping just a bit closer, pressing his arousal against her bottom.

"O-okay. I see now."

Reluctantly he let her go. "Now you have to get the chrysanthemum out of the old pot." His voice sounded strangely strained even to him. "Grab on to the plant, hold it up, tap a few times on the pot with your spade, wiggle…wiggle it around, that's it. Now gently extract the plant and root ball from the pot."

She did all this, grinning when the plant came loose. "Look at all those roots. Must be a healthy plant."

"Jock doesn't grow anything but. Those roots will have more room to spread out in their new home. Now set the root ball into the hole you made, and fill in with more potting soil."

She started to get interested in the task and forgot to worry about whether she got dirty.

"Now really mash the dirt around the base of the plant firmly." Again, he had to demonstrate, putting his arms on either side of hers, their fingers comingling in the warm, fragrant soil. They pressed enough dirt around that one plant for ten.

"Wh-what next?" Sonya's words came out a breathy hiss.

"Whatever you want." John-Michael didn't plan for that to come out. It just did, and it produced the desired result. Sonya turned slightly so that she faced him in the circle of his arms. He thought she was going to kiss him, but instead she laid her head on his shoulder. His arms went around her instinctively.

"Why is it so hard being me sometimes?"

"It's hard being anybody. It's hard being human. All the money in the world doesn't protect you from stress and heartache and disappointment and hurt."

"Hurt most of all. I don't know why I'm doing this. I know you have no interest in comforting the poor little rich girl."

"That's not true." He rubbed her back, knowing he was getting dirt on it. But she was doing the same to him, clutching at his shirt beneath the leather jacket. "We've had our differences, but deep down you know I care about you." More and more each day—as he saw depths he never imagined, compassion only hinted at in her youth.

She looked up at him, her eyes glistening with unshed tears, asking an unspoken question. He answered that question by lowering his head and capturing those sweet, pink lips with his.

Her response was instantaneous and explosive. She moved her hands to his head, pulling him closer, working her mouth against his hungrily, pressing her body against his. She hooked one leg around his, opening herself. The heat at her core radiated out against his erection.

Her hair was pulled back into a simple ponytail—she'd been wearing less elaborate hairstyles lately. He slid the elastic off, letting her hair loose, burying his hands in the soft, gold silk. He felt like a spider caught in a web, unable to extricate himself even if he wanted to.

"You do still want me," she said, almost sobbing.

"Yes. How could I not? You're the most beautiful—"

"I don't want to hear that," she said. She moved her arms around his neck and stood on her toes so she could speak softly into his ear. "Beauty doesn't last forever. So if that's all you're attracted to—"

"Sonya. I think you're beautiful inside and out. There's nothing wrong with who you are."

She resumed the kiss, even more passionately than before, and John-Michael was starting to wonder if there was anyplace close by that would make a good place for a tryst when a sound from a distance penetrated his brain. He realized fuzzily that someone had entered the greenhouse. He broke the kiss. "Someone's coming."

"I don't care." She tried to resume their heated exchange, but John-Michael forced himself to pull away.

"I do. You're engaged to another man, at least officially. I'm not going to be the one to ruin your reputation."

Sonya apparently saw the wisdom in his argument. She let him go, though she looked sullen about it, and went to work repairing her hair. John-Michael used the corner of her apron to hastily wipe a smudge from her face.

She pointed to her mouth, then his. "Lipstick," she whispered. He wiped his mouth with the back of his hands.

She took off the apron and hung it on the hook where they'd found it as footsteps and jaunty whistling grew closer. It was Jock, and as he came around the corner with a small wheelbarrow bearing some winter-dead bushes he'd apparently just pulled out of some flower bed, he stopped in surprise.

"What're you two doing in here?" he asked, curious but not sounding particularly suspicious.

"I just wanted to see what you had blooming. The roses look marvelous, Jock."

"Did you see the red-and-white-variegated one?" he asked, a kid doing show-and-tell. "It's only budding right now, but it should have some beautiful blooms..." He trailed off as he took a hard look at Sonya, then quickly looked away. "...um, that is, I was thinking of it for your bouquet," he finished lamely. Then John-Michael saw what his father had seen. A smudge, roughly the shape of a hand, along the side of Sonya's breast. In fact, she had no small amount of dirt on her sweater from his careless caresses.

"That sounds lovely," Sonya said. "I think I'll go see what Mattie has on for dinner." She headed for the door and John-Michael started to follow, but his father called him back. "A word with you please, son."

He nodded, but he stopped Sonya before she got too far and whispered in her ear, "Change your clothes." She looked down at herself, saw the hand print and blushed prettily.

Jock was busy bagging up the dead plants for disposal when John-Michael rejoined him. "You wanted something, Dad?"

"Any fool can see what you've been up to."

John-Michael had nothing to say to that. He had no

defense. Nor did he really feel he needed one. He was counting the days until seducing Sonya would no longer be forbidden.

"I thought you two got over all that stuff years ago."

"It was just a kiss."

"Damn it, John-Michael, I didn't think I raised an idiot. She belongs to another man. How could you even—"

"She doesn't. She's not going to marry Marvin."

"Oh, is that what she's tellin' ya?"

John-Michael pulled a black plastic garbage bag from the roll and helped his father dispose of the dead plants. But as soon as he picked one up, he realized they weren't dead. "Aren't these Muffy's camellias? The ones she's so fond of?"

"So what if they are?"

"She'll *kill* you for pulling these up. Dad, what were you thinking?"

"I was thinking that I'm the head gardener around here, and it's high time Miss Muffy listened to my advice. Those camellias were old and they overpowered the corner where they were growing. I'm going to put some nice azaleas there."

"Her mother planted those camellia bushes," John-Michael said, as if Jock needed reminding. "Are you trying to get yourself fired?"

Jock narrowed his eyes. "If she fires me, I'll file sexual harassment charges against her."

"Sexual—dear God! What are you talking about?"

"It doesn't concern you."

"Yes, it does. So long as I'm on the Patterson payroll, part of my job is keeping you in line."

"How can you keep me in line when you're not keeping yourself in line?" Jock shot back. "You were all over Muffy's precious daughter. You're more likely to get fired than me."

"I'm already leaving. Dad, what did Muffy do to tick you off?"

But Jock wouldn't say anything more about it.

Chapter Nine

"I hope you don't mind, Mother," Sonya said as she and Muffy sat down at the huge walnut table in the dining room. "But I asked John-Michael to join us for dinner. We have something we want to discuss with you."

"No, I don't mind," Muffy said vaguely. She'd rubbed the eyeliner off one eye. This was very un-Muffy-like.

"Mother, are you feeling all right?"

"Never better," Muffy answered too quickly. "Why do you ask?"

"Oh, I don't know. You seem a little distracted."

"I'm fine." Her smile was obviously forced. "What tasteless concoction is Mattie forcing us to eat tonight?" She lifted the silver lid off a serving dish, revealing poached salmon. "Oh, hell, not more fish! I'm going to grow gills if I eat any more fish. Why can't I have a nice, juicy steak now and then?" She made equally disparaging remarks about the steamed asparagus and wild rice as she spooned them onto her plate, leading Sonya to the unmistakable conclusion that something was bothering Muffy.

"Mother, are you going to tell me what's wrong?"

John-Michael chose that moment to enter the dining room. He'd changed into clean, pressed khakis and a long-sleeved knit shirt. There was no sign of their "dirty" kiss in the greenhouse an hour ago.

"You're late," Muffy said.

"I'm sorry." He looked at the grandfather clock in the corner, which read one minute until seven. "Sonya, you did say seven, right?"

"Yes. You're not late. We just sat down ourselves."

"Don't contradict me," Muffy said peevishly.

John-Michael shared a look with Sonya, who shrugged helplessly. She had no idea what was going on with her mother. But maybe it was better this way. If Muffy was already in a lousy mood, they couldn't ruin it with their bad news.

"What's that?" Muffy asked, nodding toward an arrangement of chrysanthemums and baby's breath that graced the center of the huge table.

"It's a flower arrangement," Sonya answered dryly.

"I know what it is. What's it doing there?"

"Just sitting, I think."

"Don't be cheeky, Sonya."

"It's one of Jock's arrangements he did specially for you," Sonya replied, trying to give her mother the answer she was looking for. Jock had been doing a fresh arrangement every day since Muffy had come home from the hospital. Mattie or June would deliver the new flowers each day to Muffy's bedroom, then take the previous day's arrangement and put it somewhere else in the house. "I think this was Saturday's delivery."

"It's ugly," she declared. "Get it out of here. I don't want to look at it."

"Ooookay." Sonya rose, walked over to the flowers, picked up the heavy ceramic container and headed toward the kitchen.

"No. Wait. Bring them back."

Sonya did a U-turn and deposited the flowers where they'd been. Then she waited to see if Muffy would reverse her orders again.

Muffy looked at Sonya, challenging. "I can change my mind if I want."

"Of course you can, Mother. Now, are you going to tell me what's really bothering you?"

Muffy burst into tears, prompting Sonya to rush around to the head of the table and put her arms around her mother. "Please, Mother, don't cry. Whatever it is, we can fix it, we can get through it together. But I can't help if you won't tell me."

"It's n-nothing," Muffy said through her tears.

John-Michael looked on, concern etched in his face. "Does this have anything to do with the camellias?" he asked.

Muffy grew very still, and her crying subsided as if by magic. "What about the camellias?" she asked, carefully enunciating every word.

"Nothing," John-Michael said hastily, but it was too late. Muffy shook off Sonya's embrace, pushed her chair out, threw her linen napkin into her plate of untouched salmon, stood and marched out of the room. Sonya and John-Michael hastily followed.

"Mrs. Patterson," John-Michael said as he pursued her through the foyer, "please forget I said anything."

"Mother, you can't go out without a coat," Sonya implored. But it was as if Muffy didn't hear them. She unlocked the dead bolt and yanked the heavy oak doors open, then tromped out into the darkness. It was chilly out, in the forties, and the rain hadn't let up. Oblivious, wearing only a thin sweater, Muffy marched across the porch, down the stairs and along a walkway to the side of the house.

There, the mansion's landscape lighting revealed the atrocity, five gaping holes where Muffy's mother's camellias had grown until recently.

"Sonya, get me a gun," Muffy said. "I'm going to kill the son of a bitch this time."

"Mother, calm down." The request was ludicrous. Though Muffy had insisted Sonya learn how to protect herself, she'd never touched a gun in her life.

"We should go back inside," John-Michael said calmly.

Muffy turned on him. "You can't save him this time, John-Michael. He deliberately went against my orders to hurt me. I'm going to fire him. I might even file criminal charges. Those camellia bushes were ancient and valuable."

"I saved the bushes," he said. "I rescued them from the garbage. I'll replant them tomorrow."

"You mean you had a hand in this?" Sonya demanded.

"No. But I caught Jock throwing them out and I knew something strange was going on. I knew your mother wouldn't agree to digging up those bushes."

"Damn straight I wouldn't!" Muffy said, and she turned and strode back toward the front porch.

"What in the hell is going on?" Sonya asked, terribly confused.

"Obviously my father and your mother fought about something."

"But they fight all the time! I've never seen Jock do something so deliberately cruel before."

"Neither have I. You take care of your mother. I'll see if I can find Jock."

Sonya found her mother standing in the foyer. Her head of steam had evaporated, and she was crying into her hands. "Come on, Mother," Sonya said. "Let's go upstairs and get out of these damp clothes. Maybe you'd like a warm bath?"

"Yes, that would be nice." Muffy allowed herself to be led upstairs to her suite, where Sonya helped her undress and wrapped her in a fluffy terry robe.

"I'll draw a bath for you."

"With some of those nice lavender bubbles," Muffy said. "Mihir says lavender would help me to sleep."

Muffy seemed calmer once she was in the bath surrounded by mountains of fragrant bubbles.

"Do you want to talk about it?" Sonya asked gently.

"No. But I mean it about firing Jock. Give him a month's severance pay and tell him to clear out tomorrow. I don't want to ever lay eyes on him again."

"Don't make any hasty decisions."

"I should have fired him years ago. Oh, Sonya, what was it you and John-Michael wanted to discuss with me?"

"Nothing important." Sonya couldn't possibly tell Muffy now that the wedding was off. The news would have to wait a little longer, until this current upset was settled.

SONYA DIDN'T LEAVE Muffy's room until she was sure her mother was asleep. Then she tiptoed out, carrying Jock's latest flower offering, a small pot of violets, with her. Muffy hadn't paid it any mind, but Sonya didn't want her mother waking up and seeing it and getting angry all over again.

John-Michael was waiting for her out in the hall. "How is she?"

"Sleeping. I took her blood pressure and listened to her heart. Everything seems normal." Dr. Cason had taught her how to do those things. "Did you find Jock?"

"There's no sign of him, but his car's still here. He might have gone for a long walk to cool off. Or, he might have walked to the nearest liquor store."

"Or to an AA meeting," she said optimistically. "He told me there's an AA meeting going on somewhere in the city at almost any hour of the day."

"We can hope. Listen, about what happened earlier—"

"John-Michael, can we not dissect it like we did last time? I'm not in the mood for apologies or blame or regrets. It happened. In fact, I'm glad it happened. I *made* it happen. And I liked it."

"I wasn't exactly an innocent bystander. I think you probably could have mashed dirt without my help."

She smiled. "For now, let's just leave it at that, okay?"

He nodded.

Sonya retreated to her own suite, but she was much too jittery to sleep. Instead, she called both Brenna and Cindy to fill them in on the latest development with Marvin. Just hearing her friends' voices made her feel better. But she was still restless. She put on an old pair of jeans and a sorority T-shirt—an outfit she normally wouldn't be caught dead in. She added some old hiking boots and a hooded rain slicker. She needed some fresh air, and she wasn't going to let the rain stop her.

She half expected John-Michael to meet her in the hallway, the way he used to do when she was younger and tried to sneak out at night. But his usually perfect radar wasn't zeroing in on her whereabouts tonight, apparently.

She could have left the estate, driven around all by herself for a change. But for some reason she didn't feel like being defiant. She didn't want to irritate John-Michael or her mother. The estate was large enough that she could walk around inside the perimeter fence. She could have her solitude and her fresh air and be safe, too.

The rain was coming down a little harder than it had been earlier, and the temperature was a bit cooler than she'd thought. Sonya pulled the hood up on her slicker and set out, past the swimming pool and tennis courts, past the gardener's cottage, all dark this late at night.

There wasn't much ambient light, but she didn't need much. She'd become familiar with every inch of the estate as a child. The artificially landscaped hills and valleys, the strategically placed boulders, had served as a perfect backdrop for her solitary games of pretend. She'd wandered off by herself a lot after her father's death. The house had been a dark, depressing place back then, and it had been easier to lose herself in fantasy, where she could be a fairy princess, a superhero or supermodel.

She had a small flashlight in her pocket, but she didn't even use it until she got to the back of the estate, where the manicured landscaping gave way to a woods of oak and cottonwood, bois d'arc and hackberry trees.

She'd played hide-and-seek by herself among these trees. She remembered one tree in particular, a fat bois d'arc that leaned over so far she could climb it like a monkey.

Wouldn't Brenna be surprised to learn Sonya had been a tomboy? She'd given up her half-savage ways the moment she'd discovered boys, makeup and nail polish, but once you learned to climb trees, you never forgot.

There was the tree. It had leaned so far over that now it was growing horizontally. Sonya brushed off the trunk and sat down. The canopy of leaves overhead protected her somewhat from the rainfall.

She could think here. More to the point, she couldn't escape thoughts of that kiss in the greenhouse. She couldn't pretend it was a fluke this time. Nor could she assign blame to John-Michael. He might have been flirting with her, but she had started the kiss.

Really, was there any need to blame anyone? A couple of weeks ago, such a kiss would have qualified as unacceptable, an aberration in her behavior and a terrible lapse in his. Now the only feeling she could muster was a sense of wonder that it had happened, that John-Michael hadn't pushed her away, that he hadn't tried to deny or minimize the chemistry between them.

For the first time in forever, she let herself anticipate something real developing between herself and her bodyguard. Her soon-to-be-ex-bodyguard. If he had a spark of feeling for her—and clearly he did—there was hope.

And she wanted it to happen. She wanted to make it happen—not with the naive expectations of a teenager, and not with the walk-on-the-wild-side mentality she'd once had. At nineteen, the only sort of relationship she had seen with John-Michael was a clandestine one. Now she could visualize something much different.

Her mother might have something to say about it. But she wasn't going to live her life by Muffy's snobbish rules any longer. She loved her mother very much, and she would do everything she could to get Muffy through the current crisis, whatever it was. And she would get through this fake-wedding thing. But then she was going to make some big changes. She could only hope John-Michael would want to be a part of them. The idea was almost too delicious to dwell on for long.

An alien noise intruded into her musings. Sonya sat up straighter and drew her slicker closer about her. Her imagination whirled with images of rabid possums and skunks. Surely there weren't any dangerous animals in the woods. The noise came again, and Sonya decided it was human in origin—a wild, jungle yell.

Trespassers? In this woods, on her family estate? No one could cross the fence without setting off an alarm. But who could it be?

Arming herself with a stick as tall as she was, just in case, Sonya slipped silently through the woods toward the noise. She would get just close enough to figure out what she was dealing with, she reasoned. If she didn't turn on the flashlight, she wouldn't be seen in the dark—her raincoat was a navy blue.

She was drawing closer to a creek that wound its way through the property. It was a good-size creek, a branch of Buffalo Bayou, and with the recent rains they'd had, it would be swollen. She could hear it rushing across rocks and tree roots.

As lightning flashed, she saw it—a man's naked torso swinging through the trees. The primal yell came again, a loud "Whoop!" And then she knew who it was, and her fear was replaced by concern and no small amount of dread at what, exactly, she would find.

When she reached him, she realized why she'd seen the body in movement. Jock McPhee was on her old tire swing, the one his son had hung for her in an effort to cheer her up after her father's death. On a hot summer day, it swung out over a place where the creek pooled into a shallow swimming hole. In the middle of winter, in a thunderstorm, the waters below the tire swing looked more like white-water rapids.

"Jock!" she yelled, trying to be heard above the rain and the rush of water. He wore only a pair of raggedy cutoff shorts. If he didn't fall into the water and get swept away, hypothermia would get him.

Jock shielded his eyes and peered in her general direction. "Someone there?"

"It's me, Sonya! Come down from that swing right now!" The tire swing was tied very high up on a long rope. Lord only knew how Jock had reached the tire in the first place. She'd never been able to reach it by herself; she'd always climbed up the tree to the "launching branch," and John-Michael had swung the tire up to her, requiring her to catch it with one hand while holding on to the tree with the other.

The tire swung in a wide arc that spanned the entire creek. The trick was to let go at just the right moment so that you fell into the deeper part of the swimming hole.

Jock hadn't let go, thank God. But the swing was slowing down. "I don't know how to get down," he called back. He sounded a little bit scared.

"Don't jump into the water," Sonya cautioned. "You just stay right there, don't move. I'll go find John-Michael."

"No! John-Michael will yell at me."

"I can't get you down by myself."

"If you leave, I might fall," he wheedled. "I'll just jump now."

"No!" A strong man with all his faculties could get swept away by the current. A drunk man—for surely Jock was drunk—didn't stand a chance. "I'll help you. Just let me think…" If she could pull the tire closer to shore, he could at least fall in a shallower area where he'd have a chance. She remembered the branch she'd been carrying for protection. It was still clutched in her hand.

Maybe it would be long enough. She climbed down the steep bank, slipping a couple of times in the mud, grazing her hand on a sharp rock. She landed in water a few inches deep. It quickly soaked into her boots, which obviously weren't waterproof, and it was bone-numbingly cold. She waded out until the water was to midcalf; any deeper and she risked having her feet swept out from under her by the current.

"Okay, Jock, I'm going to hold this branch out to you. See if you can reach it." She held the branch up and out, leaning her body out as far as she dared. Jock reached, but he was a few inches shy.

"I can't get it."

"Can you grab it between your feet?"

He did manage to hook one bare foot around the branch. Sonya pulled on the branch and caused the tire to start swinging again. Then, somehow, Jock managed to pull together enough coordination to grab the end of the branch when he came close enough. The jerk on the branch unbalanced Sonya, but she regained her footing.

"Now what?" Jock asked, totally putting his faith in her.

Oh, God, she hoped she could pull this off. "I'm going to pull the swing toward me, toward the shore. Then you're going to jump." She hoped.

Amazingly, the plan worked. Sonya pulled Jock and the tire swing only a few feet, but that was enough to clear the deepest, most hazardous part of the creek. She had the branch almost straight above her now.

"Now jump!"

Completely trusting, he did. She released the branch

and reached out to break his fall. They both landed in a tumble in the shallow water.

"Are you hurt?" Sonya asked. She was pretty sure she was okay, just cold.

"Aye, my heart's broken in two," he said on a sob.

"Now isn't the time to fall apart," she said as she stood and dragged Jock to his bare feet. Hurt or not, she had to get him out of the water and somewhere warm. His skin was cold and clammy and he was shivering uncontrollably. Now she could smell the alcohol on his breath.

He hobbled to the shore on bare feet, and she pushed and shoved and pulled him up the steep bank. Once there, he fell into a heap. "I can't go on," he said.

"Jock! The hardest part is over."

"It's just beginning," he said miserably.

Sonya took off her raincoat and gave it to Jock. Though it was a tight fit, he was able to shove his arms into the sleeves after a couple of tries. It might hold some of his body heat in. She was cold in her T-shirt, but she could stand it. "Can you stand up?"

"Just leave me here. I'm ready to meet the Lord."

"You are *not* going to meet the Lord in this shabby state. Now get on your feet. March!" She felt bad about bullying him, but she couldn't think of any other way to get him back to safety. She didn't dare leave him alone to summon help. He might just roll back into the creek.

That was when she heard something crashing through the underbrush toward them. She'd lost her stick. She groped around for something to use as a weapon. Just as her hand closed over a rock, John-Michael strode into view, drenching wet.

"Dad?"

Thank God. "He's in a bad way, John-Michael. We have to get him warm. I think he might be suffering from hypothermia."

"Sonya, what are you doing here?" But even as he asked, he was hauling his father to his feet in a way that indicated to Sonya he'd done it a time or two before. "Come on, Dad," he said gently, not angry as Jock had predicted, though the anger might come later once Jock was out of danger.

Between them they were able to walk Jock back to the gardener's cottage. The Patterson estate had never seemed so large, the distances so vast as they did that night while they inched toward their goal. Finally they were inside the door, which, thank goodness, Jock never locked. John-Michael flipped on the lights and cranked up the heat.

The cottage was neat as a starched white shirt—except for the debris sitting on the coffee table in the living room. An empty bottle of Johnny Walker, a half-empty flask of peppermint schnapps, and several empty cans of Old Milwaukee, all testament to the binge.

"Jeez, Dad…"

"Let's get him into a warm shower," Sonya said. Recriminations could come later.

"I can handle this," John-Michael said. "I've done it before."

Sonya was being dismissed. But rather than feel affronted, she saw what was happening. John-Michael was embarrassed, humiliated, by his father's behavior.

She didn't argue with him. She simply said, "I'll help you get him to the bathroom."

Jock was singing now, some Irish ditty. He clearly wasn't feeling any physical pain, but that didn't mean he was out of danger. They lugged him to the bathroom and tugged Sonya's raincoat off him.

"Is this your coat?"

"Yes. He needed it worse than me."

John-Michael turned on warm water in the shower and dragged Jock into the stall still wearing his cutoff shorts. He quieted down when the hot water hit him. "Ah, that feels good," he murmured.

Sonya retreated from the bathroom, allowing Jock some privacy. She went into his bedroom, found a pair of clean pajamas and laid them out on the bed, which was neatly made up with fluffy pillows and a down comforter. Jock was quite a fastidious man when he wasn't drinking.

She felt terrible about him falling off the wagon. Something awful must have happened between him and Muffy. Jock had said something about his heart being broken. Was it possible he'd been carrying a torch for his employer? She thought about all the beautiful flower arrangements he'd created for Muffy during her recovery, and considered that it might be true. And maybe he'd finally gotten the courage to say something, and Muffy had shot him down.

But why, then, had Muffy been so distraught?

Chapter Ten

When John-Michael judged that his father had had enough of the hot shower, he turned off the water and handed him a huge, fluffy blue towel. Jock was alert enough to daub at himself with the towel and rub his hair with it, then wrap it around his shoulders.

"Are you okay, Dad?" John-Michael asked.

"Yeah."

"'Cause I have half a mind to take you to the hospital. With all you drank, then almost freezing yourself to death—"

"I'm okay. Can't a man get drunk without causing a national emergency?"

"You could have died, you idiot. Don't you realize that?"

"She'd have been sorry, then," he murmured.

Muffy. He didn't imagine he was going to get the whole story out of Jock tonight. But tomorrow he intended to get to the bottom of it. As if that would do any good. His days as the Patterson gardener were over. He wondered if all this was some kind of unconscious attempt on Jock's part to keep John-Michael here, prevent him from taking an outside job and leaving the fold.

It wasn't going to work. But John-Michael was going to have to figure out what to do with his father.

Jock was walking more or less under his own power, though leaning heavily on John-Michael during the short walk to his bedroom. The bed had been turned down, pajamas laid out—Sonya's doing. He felt a swelling of warmth around his heart for all that Sonya had done. He'd seen no sign of the spoiled princess tonight. He didn't know exactly what had happened, but it seemed to him that Sonya had risked her own safety to save his father.

After climbing into pajamas, Jock flopped onto the bed and, after a couple of attempts, managed to shove his feet under the covers. He dropped onto the pillows, and John-Michael saw how old he looked.

"I'm sorry," Jock murmured, his eyes awash in tears. "Do you hate your old man, John-Michael?"

"Of course I don't hate you, Dad. You made a mistake, that's all. No one's perfect."

"She'll fire me."

"We'll talk about it tomorrow." Maybe, John-Michael thought, if he managed to replant the camellias, Muffy would give Jock one more chance.

He left his father gently snoring and found Sonya sitting on a plastic bag on the sofa, so as not to get the furniture wet. She had her arms wrapped around herself, and she was shivering. It hadn't occurred to him that Jock might not be the only one in danger of hypothermia.

"Is he okay?" she asked.

John-Michael nodded. "But you're not. You need to get out of those wet clothes."

She nodded.

"You can use the shower at my place. It's closer." Which was a thinly disguised excuse to keep her close to him. He wanted to find out exactly what had happened. But he also just couldn't get enough of looking at her, this strange, bedraggled creature who, in a previous incarnation, had been unable to go five minutes without powdering her nose.

They walked along a stone path, lovingly landscaped with a rose arbor arching above it. The grass had been trimmed around the stepping stones, and soft lights peering unobtrusively from behind shrubs and at the bases of live oak trees allowed them to see where they were going.

"So what happened?" he asked. "How did you end up out in the woods with my father?"

"It was pure luck. I went for a walk to clear my head, to try to make sense of Muffy and Jock…and you and me," she added, sounding embarrassed. "Anyway, I heard this Tarzan yell…"

As the story unfolded, John-Michael's surprise grew, along with his respect. The method she'd used for pulling Jock close enough that he could save himself wasn't rocket science, but he probably wouldn't have thought of it.

"You could have gotten hurt yourself."

"I know, but I didn't feel I had a choice. I couldn't leave him alone, not even long enough to summon help. You aren't going to yell at me about this, are you?"

"Yell at you?" Far from it. He wanted to wrap his arms around her in gratitude for saving his father's life at the risk of her own. What kind of woman would do that? Certainly not a spoiled, self-absorbed one.

It wasn't far to John-Michael's apartment atop the five-car garage. Truly, though, his place wasn't any closer than Sonya's suite would have been. He walked her up the stairs, wondering how messy his place was. He was nowhere as obsessively neat as Jock, though he didn't live in complete chaos, either.

When they entered through the kitchen, John-Michael was relieved to see no piles of dirty dishes in the sink of clothes lying around on the floor. The service that took care of housekeeping in the main house also took a swipe at his place every couple of weeks—one of the perks of working for Muffy.

"You can use the shower first," he said, though he hoped she didn't take too long.

"Thank you." But she made no move for the bathroom. Instead she looked around the place, her eyes taking in everything. "I haven't been in here for a long time. I think the last time I saw your apartment, you still had heavy-metal band posters on the walls and motorcycle parts on the living room floor."

"I still have an Ozzy Osbourne poster in my bedroom." Ouch. He wished he hadn't mentioned his bedroom.

"Not quite as grown-up as you pretend to be, huh?"

"Would you just go take your shower?"

She reached out a hand and took his. "Why don't you take it with me?"

Her request was so straightforward, so lacking in pretense or coquettish seduction, that he nearly fell over from the force of it. He squeezed her hand as a whoosh of breath left his chest. He couldn't. Could he? Earlier today, he'd sure been thinking he could.

She must have seen his indecision, because she smiled encouragingly. "Could we just forget about all the stupid stuff, for once? Forget the master-servant roles our parents have brainwashed us with, and just be together?"

He wanted that, more than anything, right this moment. But the habit of delaying gratification was so ingrained in him, he found it difficult to throw caution and prudence out the window.

"If it's not what you want, just say so," Sonya said, far too reasonably. "But hurry up and decide. I'm freezing."

He let go of her hand, shrugged out of his soggy leather jacket and dropped it, his gaze never leaving hers. She took a sharp breath, and her pupils dilated, giving her eyes a dark, mysterious look.

"I hope you like plain ol' Dial soap," he said as he took her in his arms. Her lips were cool to the touch, but they warmed up fast enough as the kiss ignited a bonfire that warmed them both faster than the shower they'd been talking about.

John-Michael walked her backward all the way to the bathroom. He didn't bother turning on the lights. The hundred-watt bulbs that were indispensable when he was shaving would be unwelcome now. Instead he left the door open so the light from the hallway gave the room just enough definition that they wouldn't run into the walls. Still kissing Sonya, he opened the glass doors on the tub enclosure and turned on the hot water.

As the kiss heated up, Sonya went to work on the buttons of his denim shirt. Much as he liked the romantic notion of them undressing each other, with their wet clothes it would take forever. He set Sonya away from him, mourning the loss of warmth as he quickly stripped off his clothes and shoes. Taking his cue, Sonya did the same, hopping on one foot as she tugged at her wet jeans.

"This part always looks more romantic in the movies," she said, her voice oddly hoarse.

Taking pity, he helped her with the T-shirt, which clung tenaciously to her. When all that remained of her clothing was her bra and panties, it finally occurred to her to feel shy. She hesitated, and her reticence caught him right in the solar plexus.

This was Sonya. Sonya Patterson was standing in front of him in her underwear, and he was naked. His desire overcame the cold, overcame all second thoughts that might have arisen, any common sense that tried to seep into his consciousness.

He pulled her to him, wrapped his arms around her, and unhooked her bra. "You can change your mind."

"Oh, no. I've been fantasizing about this since I was fifteen. And if you even think about changing yours, so help me, McPhee, I'll break every bone in your body."

He laughed as he slid the bra straps down her arms and off. Her bare breasts were all the more intriguing to him because they were mostly in shadow. He cupped his hands around them and lightly brushed her nipples with his thumbs, and her whole body shuddered. Her nipples were already hard from the cold. He wanted to take one in his mouth and suckle. But the steam from the shower drifted out, enveloping them, reminding them how nice the warm water would feel.

John-Michael slid his hands down Sonya's torso then down her hips, taking her tiny wisp of silk panties with them.

"I'm naked," she said, her voice full of wonder, as if she'd just made a surprising discovery.

"So you are," he said with a low chuckle as he led her into the shower.

He let her stand in the spray. She emitted a groan at the pleasurable feeling. John-Michael squirted some shampoo into his hand and lathered her hair. The long, golden strands had always intrigued him. He buried his hands in the soapy, silky mass, massaging her scalp with his fingertips, and she groaned in pleasure.

She tipped her head back to rinse the suds from her hair. While she did that, he found his uninspiring deodorant soap and worked up a lather in his hands, then rubbed Sonya from her neck to pearly-pink-polished toes. She reached up to hold onto the shower nozzle for support as he let his fingers flirt with her femininity.

"Oh, John-Michael, don't."

"Don't?"

"Don't end it too quickly."

"That goes double for you." And he handed her the soap. They changed positions, and she soaped him up just as he'd done for her. She saved his most sensitive areas for last, but by the time she touched his arousal, his anticipation was so high that he nearly exploded then and there.

"Whoa."

"Mmm."

He grabbed her hand. "I think that's enough showering. The water's starting to go cold." He turned off the faucets, opened the glass doors, found a couple of towels.

He barely let Sonya daub at herself with the towel before he grabbed her up in his arms and headed for the bedroom. There was no more talking. They had a common goal in mind, and clearly Sonya did not need any more niceties. John-Michael managed to hold himself together long enough to protect Sonya from any unintended results. Then he spread her legs and entered, slowly at first. She was tight, and she gasped at the intrusion. He was afraid he'd hurt her until she tilted her hips up and took him even more deeply, sighing with deep satisfaction as he filled her.

He'd never felt anything like it. She made every other woman he'd ever had fade into obscurity, and he was positive he would never be the same after this, never be satisfied with ordinary sex again.

Their dance of intimacy didn't last long. They'd worked themselves up to such a froth in the shower that it didn't take much stimulation to send Sonya into a frenzy of writhing and uninhibited cries of ecstasy. As soon as he felt her climax, John-Michael was there, too. His entire consciousness became focused into one area of his body, until the rest didn't exist.

When it was over, they both lay panting on top of John-Michael's down comforter—a Christmas present from Muffy a few years ago, he recalled with a pinprick of guilt. But, no, he wasn't going to regret this. He might pay for it in unpleasant ways, but he wasn't going to regret it.

They didn't speak for a very long time. Sonya snuggled up against him, her head on his shoulder, and breathed long, soft breaths against his skin. He rolled the edge of the comforter over her and let her sleep. He tried to sleep himself, but he was so overcome by all that had happened that his mind wouldn't shut down. Muffy, his father, the camellia bushes, his father—again—and Sonya, incredible, delightful Sonya, who didn't want to think about tomorrow.

He was willing to let her sleep as long as she wanted to, but she awoke after a couple of hours. "Oh," she said muzzily. "I fell asleep. How rude."

"I don't mind that you did."

She pushed up on one elbow, and he could almost see the memories of all that had occurred that night filtering back into her consciousness.

She peered at the glowing green numbers of his bedside clock. "Oh, it's late. I have to go."

"Why?"

"I have to check on my mother."

"At four in the morning? She'll be fast asleep."

"I know, but I'm really worried about her. And you should check on Jock, too."

Okay, now he got it. Sonya had been full of brave words in the greenhouse, but she didn't want anyone to know she'd been with him all this time, alone in his quarters. The realization felt like a kick in the gut.

"Yeah, it would be better if you sneaked back into the house now, before anyone sees where you've spent most of the night."

She stiffened and moved away from him. "I wasn't thinking anything even close to that." She sat up all the way, holding the comforter over her breasts. It was dark enough in the bedroom he couldn't see much, anyway. But he did catch the glisten of tears in her eyes. "You're going to make this into something ugly."

"No. Not ugly. Never that. But definitely not something that can withstand the light of day."

She looked angry. Well, hell, was he supposed to let her get away with this and not challenge her? Then again, could he really blame her for how she'd been raised?

He'd been a complete fool to even *think* a wealthy debutante could fall in love with him. But he wasn't going to let her know that he'd had expectations—or see how she'd hurt him.

"I'm trying to be practical here," he said. "I caught a glimpse of the Promised Land, but it's not a place I can enter and stay indefinitely. I know that."

"McPhee, you don't know squat." She shrugged off his attempted farewell caress and threw herself out of his bed, practically stomping her way to the door.

"Sonya—"

"That's 'Miss Patterson' to you," she called from the hallway. He heard the sound of damp clothing being tugged on. "If you're going to insist on throwing out this class-distinction crap, let's be consistent."

He jumped out of bed and grabbing the first clothing he could lay his hands on, a pair of sweatpants. "Wait a minute. How can you throw this back on me? Who's the one sneaking out of bed in the middle of the night?"

"I'm not sneaking." He followed her into the living room, where she threw open his front door. Then she took a deep breath and shouted at the top of her lungs, "I slept with John-Michael! I had sex with—"

He yanked her inside and slammed the door. "Are you nuts? Do you really want to announce to the world that you slept with me when you're in the middle of planning a wedding with someone else?"

"Yes I do," she said. "But apparently you'd prefer it if I didn't. You didn't even wait until we were out of bed before picking a fight with me, so you wouldn't have to face the possibility of, God forbid, a real relationship." She pulled the front door open again. "If you don't feel the same way, then fine. Just tell me. I'll survive, just like I survived ten years ago. But don't try and blame it on fate or society or class disparity or family pressure. I want us to be together. It's not something I want to hide or be ashamed of. So if we end up *not* together, the fault falls squarely on your shoulders. Just be very clear about that."

He was so shocked by her outburst, all he could do was gape at her like a landed fish. How had this conversation gotten so out of control, so fast? He'd had her. He'd had everything he ever dreamed of in a woman, right in his bed. And then he'd blown it by letting his insecurities get the better of him.

Deep down, had he suspected all along that Sonya would reject him? Had he been looking for any sign of that rejection, jumping unfairly on the slightest signal that she didn't take him seriously?

He wanted to reassure her that he didn't take lightly the fact they'd made love. It had just happened a little ahead of his timetable, and he hadn't been prepared for it. When he'd been closest to realizing his dreams, he'd choked. He'd blown it, too afraid to really believe his dreams could become real.

Too afraid to face disappointment if he was wrong.

But by the time he formulated any words that would make sense, she was gone.

MUFFY WAS SLEEPING SOUNDLY when Sonya checked on her. She was glad, because if her mother had been awake, Sonya was afraid she would have collapsed against her and cried as she'd done when she was a little girl. Any such display would have required explanation. And while she wanted to tell her mother all that was going on, she couldn't burden Muffy with her own heartaches.

Sonya went to her own suite, but she didn't think she would be able to sleep. She changed out of her damp clothes into a comforting flannel gown, soft with many washings. She'd teased Brenna when she'd worn something equally disreputable during their road trip, she recalled. She'd been too hard on Brenna.

Sonya slept fitfully, waking at the first sign of dawn. She showered again, dried her hair and pulled it back into a ponytail. Styling it required too much energy.

Wearing faded jeans and an old, purple-striped polo shirt, she padded in sock feet down to Muffy's suite and peeked in the door. Muffy was still sleeping. Sonya slipped inside. She would wait, so Muffy wouldn't have to wake up alone.

She looked around the room for something to read— her mother always kept fashion and decorating magazines in a basket by her bed. But her gaze landed on several pieces of paper spread out over Muffy's bed. They were letters, she realized. Hand-written letters on plain white stationery, yellowed with age. The frayed ribbon they'd been tied with lay unfurled nearby.

Love letters? From her father, perhaps. Maybe that was why Muffy was so sensitive last night. She'd been thinking about her husband. Paul Patterson had been prospecting for oil in South America when he'd been kidnapped by some self-styled rebel group. They'd demanded a million-dollar ransom, which Muffy had gladly paid. Then, for unknown reasons, they'd killed him anyway.

Even after all these years, Muffy could work herself up if she let herself think about it. Perhaps she'd done just that. Jock had happened upon her unwittingly and had said something that set her off.

That made sense, Sonya thought. Except that the handwriting on the letters was not her father's.

Sonya closed her eyes, unwilling to snoop anymore. This was none of her business, and she was decidedly uncomfortable at the thought of her mother having feelings for anyone other than her father.

She tiptoed toward the door and had almost gained

the freedom of the hallway when her mother called out to her.

She turned. "Good morning, Mother."

Muffy scrubbed her face with her hand. "I acted like a complete fool last night, didn't I?"

"It was going around. What you did was nothing compared to what Jock McPhee did."

Muffy looked startled. "What did he do? Besides tear out my camellias."

"Got stinking drunk," Sonya answered matter-of-factly, "ran around in the woods in the rain, half-naked, played on the tire swing and almost fell into the creek and drowned himself. Whatever you said to him, it really set him off."

"Oh, no. He promised!"

"Don't be too hard on him, Mother. It must be so difficult for him. He was doing really well before this. You aren't really going to fire him, are you?"

"I told him if he was caught drinking again, I would."

"You could pay for him to go to a treatment facility," Sonya suggested. "He's not beyond help."

"I've offered before."

"Maybe he'll do it this time. If you tell him he can come back here when he completes the program."

"Oh, honey, I don't know if he'll even want to come back. After the things we said to each other."

Sonya sat on the edge of her mother's bed and took her hand. "What happened?"

Muffy glanced at the letters, then back at Sonya, and all at once, Sonya understood. "You and *Jock?*"

"It happened a long time ago," Muffy hastily explained. "Before I'd even met your father. We were just teenagers. His mother was the cook here. He grew up here, and we played together as children, much as you and John-Michael did. But at one point we discovered a new game, if you know what I mean."

Sonya clamped her hand over her mouth to prevent a shocked outburst from erupting. Her mother and *Jock McPhee?*

"We were so in love. The kind that's so intense it causes physical pain. Have you ever felt that kind of love, Sonya?"

Sonya nodded. She knew exactly what Muffy meant. Nothing was as exhilarating—or as painful—as your first love.

"I went away to college. We wrote to each other every day. But my roommate found out my mysterious lover's identity, and she made me see how impossible it was. I would never have been allowed to date him, much less marry him. It just wasn't done. This was back in the sixties, remember. I wanted to rebel, but in the end I toed the line. I met your father, and I wrote a Dear John letter to Jock. It was horribly insensitive of me, but I was young and stupid."

Sonya was struck dumb by this revelation. Her mother's situation hadn't been so different from hers. She'd fallen in love with an employee's son, too. Only, unlike Jock, John-Michael never wrote love letters. He'd never loved her as Jock apparently had loved Muffy. Still didn't.

"I want you to know, Sonya, that I loved your father. And I was always faithful to him, and faithful to his memory after he died. But my heart never failed to do a little flip-flop every time I saw Jock. Maybe that's why we always fought. I was afraid if we didn't fight, we'd do something else."

Sonya was familiar with that feeling.

"Recently things had started to change. Maybe it was when you became engaged, and I felt I was losing the only family I had left. Maybe it was all the romance in the air. I don't know. But after the heart attack, I realized what was truly important to me. Jock and I…"

"You don't have to tell me this part," Sonya said hastily. She wasn't comfortable thinking about her mother as a sexual being.

"Are you shocked?"

"Frankly, yes. But only because I never saw it coming. Maybe I was so caught up in my own little dramas, I wasn't paying attention."

"We didn't—that is, things hadn't gotten too far. But they were heading that way. And if I hadn't put the brakes on, well…"

"Yes, I understand."

"Jock didn't. He thought I was ashamed to be seen with him, that I thought I was too good for him. But it wasn't that at all. I just didn't think the time was right to announce our relationship to the whole world. Not right before your wedding. Is it wrong to want to take things more slowly? I'm not ready for sex! Of course, he thought thirty-something years was enough to wait. Typical man."

"Whoa, Mother. Too much information."

"It had nothing to do with money or Jock's station,"

Muffy continued, ignoring Sonya's interruption. "But he jumped to all the wrong conclusions."

"Just like his son," Sonya murmured. John-Michael had misinterpreted her wanting to leave before dawn, jumping to the conclusion that she wanted to hide what they'd done, when all along he was the one who thought they should hide it like some sordid secret.

"What? What did John-Michael do?"

Sonya hadn't thought her mother was paying a bit of attention to her, or she'd never have even breathed those words.

"He assumes I'm a snob. That I would never consider..." She stopped. Talk about too much information. Her mother was in crisis. It was no time to bring up her own silly soap opera.

Muffy looked surprised. "Is there something going on with you two?"

"Yes," she said miserably. "And no."

"What about Marvin?" Muffy asked fearfully.

Sonya decided she'd put off the unpleasant task long enough. Maybe this wasn't the ideal opportunity, but it appeared the ideal opportunity wasn't going to come along.

"There is no Marvin," she said. "He dumped me. Not only that, he stole money from me, took my jewelry and some fur coats. I've been avoiding telling you because of your heart."

"Oh, my poor baby!" Muffy threw her arms around Sonya and dragged Sonya's head to her breast, as if she were a child.

Sonya let her. "I've gotten over it, Mother. He was scum, and I didn't really love him, anyway."

"We've got to call in the authorities," Muffy said. "I know the chief of police—"

"The FBI is already looking for him. I'm not the first woman he's fleeced. I'm so sorry about the wedding. I know you were having fun planning it."

"Oh, that's all right. We can unplan things."

"Yes we can. But I was sort of hoping…" Sonya explained about Marvin contacting her, and the ruse she and John-Michael had devised for flushing Marvin out of hiding.

"So we have to pretend the wedding's on?" Muffy asked, dismayed.

"Just for a short while—if it's okay with you. You're the one paying." Sonya was glad her mother had been distracted from the subject of her and John-Michael. She didn't want to explain further what was going on, when she was so confused about it herself.

"Well, if it will help put that horrid man behind bars, I guess we can pretend the wedding's still on."

"Thanks, Mother."

A short while later, Sonya made a conference call to Cindy and Brenna. "Change of plans, girls. I'm afraid I can't go to Boston after all. I have a wedding to plan, you know."

Chapter Eleven

In Jock's quarters, John-Michael cooked bacon and eggs for breakfast. His father dragged himself out of bed, showered, dressed and joined him at the table. He was sober, but he looked like hell.

"Thanks for doing this," Jock said. "I don't deserve—"

"Let's not throw the blame and guilt around this time, okay?" John-Michael cut in. After Sonya's abrupt departure from his bed a few hours ago, he wasn't in a very tolerant mood. "We have to figure out what to do. First thing, we have to replant the camellia bushes. Second, you have to apologize to Muffy. Third, you have to agree to go through a substance abuse treatment program."

"And don't I have any say?"

"If you want to continue with your job here—"

"I don't. I'll be moving out as soon as I find another position. Tootsie Milford has tried to steal me away from Muffy often enough. She'll take me on."

John-Michael was shocked into silence. This was

the first time he'd ever heard Jock entertain the idea that he could possibly survive anywhere other than the Patterson estate.

"I think Muffy could be persuaded to take you—"

"Confound it, boy, don't you listen? I don't want to work for Muffy anymore. And if you knew what she'd done, you wouldn't expect it of me."

"What did she do?" John-Michael was now more curious than anything.

"She toyed with my affections."

"What?"

"She led me to believe she returned my feelings."

"Wait a minute. You have some kind of crush on—"

"A crush?" Jock thundered. "We were in love! At least, I was, and I thought she was, too. But she lost her nerve. Didn't want us to be seen together. She had a lot of pretty words about how she'd changed her priorities, and she realized how wrong she'd been all those years ago to break off with me—"

"You and *Muffy?*"

"What, you don't think I'm good enough for the likes of her?"

John-Michael didn't know what to think. For the moment he returned to practicalities. "Are you sure you want to work for Tootsie? She's a tyrant, from what her other employees have said. You could come live with me for a while, till you find something better." He'd already rented a house within easy driving distance of the Wallisville Substation, where his first posting would be when he started with the Sheriff's Department next month.

"I'm sure I can work things out with Tootsie. You've taken care of me long enough."

"What about going into a treatment program?"

"I'll stick with AA," Jock mumbled. "It was working for me. I already called my sponsor. He's going to meet with me, and we're going to talk about what happened and how I could make better choices next time. In the end it comes down to me, doesn't it?"

John-Michael nodded.

"I won't disappoint you again. I mean it, John-Michael. Once I get away from this place, and I don't have to see *her* every day, the pain won't be so bad."

"Won't you miss this place?" John-Michael asked. He knew he would. "We've never lived anywhere else."

"Aye, I'll miss it. But we're better off somewhere else—both of us. If you know what's good for you, you'll stay away from Sonya Patterson, too. I've no doubt she has a good heart. She might even be in love with you. But no good can come of our kind mixing with theirs. If she were to pair off with you, her mother would likely never speak to her again."

John-Michael had long ago considered that possibility. One of the many reasons a liaison between himself and Sonya was hopeless.

"Sonya would be cut off without a cent," Jock continued. "And while I've no doubt you could provide for the girl, put a roof over her head and food on the table, that isn't enough for someone born to wealth. She would come to resent not having the fine things she's used to."

John-Michael had considered that, too. Even if she worked—even if she got a job as an engineer—they wouldn't earn enough to live in a big fancy house, drive luxury cars and employ domestic workers.

He didn't bother denying that there was anything between himself and Sonya.

"I hear you," John-Michael said.

Jock finished off his toast and marmalade. "I'm going to call Tootsie. She's given me her number often enough."

John-Michael hoped his father wasn't jumping out of the frying pan and into the fire.

SONYA DIDN'T SEE John-Michael again until that afternoon, when she had an appointment with the florist. But she was feeling surprisingly upbeat as she and Muffy waited in the back of the limo for John-Michael to appear. She was so relieved to have admitted the truth to her mother. And Muffy had taken the whole thing surprisingly well. She'd already begun to have her doubts about Marvin, about his exceedingly long absence and the fact he hadn't come to be at his future bride's side when her mother had been stricken ill. If he wasn't willing to put his family first now, how would he be after a few years of marriage?

"I'm afraid we've wasted more money on this non-existent wedding than he stole from me," Sonya had said. But Muffy had waved away her daughter's concerns. "It's only money. And after we catch him, we'll be heroes!" She'd been so enthralled with the idea that they would be helping the FBI that she'd forgotten her own heartbreak for a while, or at least had allowed herself to be distracted from it.

"You know," Muffy said as they waited for John-

Michael, "a lot of the wedding plans won't be wasted, really. We'll keep the file, with all the choices about colors and flowers and cakes, and when you decide to get married again, a lot of the work will be done."

"Yes, that's true," Sonya said, forcing a smile, trying to look on the bright side for her mother's sake. She didn't have the heart to tell Muffy she didn't think she would ever want to plan another fancy wedding. Surviving this three-ring circus once in a lifetime was enough.

John-Michael trotted out to the limo, saw Sonya and Muffy in the back and elected to ride up front with Tim. Sonya couldn't blame him.

"I hope John-Michael doesn't think I paint him with the same brush as I do his father," Muffy whispered.

"Why not? They're cut from the same cloth," Sonya said. "Both stubborn as mules and carrying chips on their shoulders the size of Mount Rushmore."

"Well, I don't blame him for anything that's happened. In fact, I'm very grateful for all he's done for me over the years. I'll miss him terribly when he moves on."

Sonya swallowed hard. She didn't want to think about that. "Won't you miss Jock, too?"

"Ooooooh, don't get me started on Jock." Muffy crossed her arms and set her jaw.

"Maybe you should talk to him. Explain everything just like you did to me."

"You can't explain anything to Jock. He assumes everything I say is a slight. Next thing you know, he'll get mad and chop down the live oak tree."

"He and John-Michael replanted the camellias, you know."

"I know." She looked at Sonya with tears in her eyes. "I deeply regret not finding out what Jock and I could have been together, all those years ago. Our lives would have been very different. But it might have been really, really good."

"But what about Daddy?" Sonya suddenly felt very young, mourning her father all over again.

"I don't regret your father, and without him I couldn't have had you. But still…"

Sonya wished she could think of something that would ease her mother's pain. But she wasn't exactly brilliant where relationships were concerned. Her own love life was a complete disaster. The man she loved had only wanted to get her into bed, and was throwing up every road block he could think of so he wouldn't have to admit that he didn't feel the same as Sonya did. She'd left the ball in his court. And he hadn't even picked it up, much less returned it.

"It's too late for Jock and me," Muffy said. "Too much water under the bridge. But it's not too late for you. Promise me you'll always follow your heart. You should never have settled for Marvin, even if your silly mother was over-the-moon about him."

"Following your heart doesn't work when the man you love doesn't love you back."

"Are we talking about anyone specific?" Muffy's eyes, alive with curiosity, showed no trace of the tears that had threatened a few moments earlier.

"Who do you think?" She glanced up toward the front seat. Though the soundproof glass was up, she didn't trust John-Michael not to read lips in the mirror.

"You're in love with John-Michael!"

"Shh! I've been in love with him since I was ten! But he was always more loyal to you than hot for me. I gave him plenty of chances."

"Sonya!"

"Oh, don't you go all sanctimonious on me! Like mother, like daughter, don't you think?"

Muffy put her hand over her mouth, and Sonya wasn't sure if she was delighted or horrified.

"I can't believe you're that shocked. You knew I had a crush on him."

"When you were a teenager, yes. That was why I hired John-Michael to protect you. I knew he wouldn't betray the trust I put in him. But I thought you outgrew that long ago."

"Unfortunately, no."

"Have you…made your feelings known?"

"I slept with him." Sonya's face burned. "He can't handle the fact that I'm rich and he's not. Or that's the excuse he's tossing out. I think he just doesn't feel anything for me."

"Don't you dare start crying," Muffy said urgently. "Tim can see everything in his mirror."

"Tell me a joke, then."

"I think I'll give all my money to charity."

Sonya laughed.

"Maybe that shouldn't be a joke."

"WHAT ARE THEY DOING?" John-Michael asked Tim. "I can't see without turning around."

"There's a lot of grimacing and gesturing going on

back there," Tim replied. "Sonya's blushing. Oh, now they're laughing and now they're hugging."

John-Michael had a very bad feeling about this. It sounded as if Sonya might be confiding in her mother. And though John-Michael was no longer dependent on Muffy for a job or a place to live, he didn't want to leave her employ on bad terms, as his father was. Even now Jock was packing up his belongings and preparing to move into Tootsie's servants' quarters.

Tim had the good manners not to ask what was going on that had the house in such an uproar. But, as observant as Tim was, he probably knew everything.

Jasmine Florist's Shop was in the Houston suburb of Sugarland. They had other locations closer to River Oaks, where the Pattersons lived, but Muffy preferred to visit the original location, which was connected to a huge greenhouse. All the ritzy ladies of Houston came out here to personally stroll through the climate-controlled greenhouse and pick out the exact hues they wanted for their important arrangements. Sometimes they would even pick out the exact blooms.

Muffy was armed with swatches of fabrics—bridesmaid dresses, ribbons from their hair pieces and even samples of the church's carpeting—to give master florist Mitchell Kelloran the inspiration for the bouquets and other arrangements.

Sonya had told Muffy this morning that the actual wedding wouldn't be happening. That might have been what they were discussing in the back of the limo. He hoped that was it. Anyway, Muffy had spoken to him a couple of hours ago, insisting that she was all in favor of carrying on with the wedding plans until they caught "that slime-sucking slug." She'd also apologized for her "emotional upheaval" of the previous night, and had declared she felt just fine this morning, well enough to accompany Sonya to the florist.

So here they were. As Sonya stepped out of the limo, she avoided John-Michael's gaze. He could have been invisible, for all the notice she gave him. Muffy, on the other hand, looked at him with her mouth puckered as if she'd just sucked a lemon.

Sonya had told her, all right.

He hated to think that after all these years, his relationship with Muffy would go sour. She'd always had a soft spot for him, the poor little motherless boy. Would he from this point forward be "that gardener's son who seduced my daughter and left her high and dry"?

Maybe if he talked to her, made her understand that he was doing what was best for Sonya…no, that would never work. He couldn't face Muffy if she knew he and Sonya had made love. No matter what the circumstances, she wouldn't approve.

He watched from a distance as Sonya oohed and ahhed over the sketches the snooty florist showed her of his "vision" for her wedding. Then he followed at a discreet distance as they walked the aisles of the greenhouse, and Mr. Kelloran held up various blooms against Sonya's skin to see how well they complemented her golden-ivory tones.

Sonya was a damn fine actress. No one would guess she wasn't head-over-heels about Marvin and breathlessly excited about the upcoming nuptials. And Muffy was no slouch. She played the interfering mama to the hilt.

John-Michael thought he was pretty good at hiding his feelings. He even thought he might like to work undercover someday. But he found it hard to hide his feelings where Sonya was concerned. Watching her play the blushing bride, even when he knew it was all a sham, hurt more today than ever.

He couldn't stop thinking about it, about how she'd given herself to him last night and how much he'd liked it and how much he wanted her again…and how impossible it all was. She might actually have feelings for him. But one of them had to pull his head out of the clouds. Look at what unrequited love for Muffy had done to his father.

He wasn't going to end up like that, wasting his life waiting for a grain of attention, reliant on Sonya's whims, feeling destroyed if she dated someone else, married someone else. He needed to get away before that happened.

"DON'T LOOK NOW," Sonya said under her breath, "but Tootsie's right over on the next aisle."

"Where?" Muffy asked, peering through the screen of bougainvillea vines. "Why wouldn't you want to see Tootsie?"

"I was completely horrible to her when you were sick. But she would have worn you to a frazzle with her 'concern' when you were supposed to be getting your rest."

"Tootsie can be a tad exhausting," Muffy agreed.

"I'm sure you did the right thing. And I'm sure she doesn't hold it against you."

"Oh, Mother, Tootsie holds it against me that I was born. She can't stand me."

"Don't be ridiculous. Oh, there she is." Muffy waved to her friend.

Tootsie, of course, scurried right over. "Oh, sugar, I'm so glad I ran into you!" She air-kissed Muffy and gave Sonya a tepid smile. "I can't thank you enough."

"For what?" Muffy asked, bewildered.

"Why, for finally letting go of your gardener! I must say, it was very selfish of you to keep Jock McPhee to yourself all these years. I'm here to get some fresh ideas for my patio. I want all the old stuff ripped out."

To her credit, Muffy recovered quickly from the shock. "Well, he's certainly good at ripping things out. You've hired him, then?"

"He asked me for the job, and I'd have been crazy to turn him down. He's the best landscaper in all of Houston. What possessed you to let him leave? I know Sonya's wedding must be a huge financial burden for you." She paused to give Sonya a deprecating scowl.

Sonya fully expected Muffy to blurt out that Jock was a loose cannon, a drunk who'd delivered one too many nasty surprises. Instead, Muffy smiled. "Sometimes a man needs a change of scenery. I'm sure it gets boring, taking care of the same old house and yard all the time. He wanted a new challenge, and I fully supported his decision."

Tootsie narrowed her eyes suspiciously. "He says you fired him."

Muffy shrugged. "Technically, I did. But I would call it more of a mutual decision. I'm sorry, Tootsie, but we really need to be moving on. We have another appointment all the way downtown. I hope everything works out with you and Jock. I'm sure he'll enjoy the challenge. Come, Sonya."

Sonya gave Tootsie her best superior-ice-queen smile, then hustled her mother to the limo parked right outside the greenhouse door.

Muffy held it together until Tim and John-Michael were inside and all the doors were closed. Then she lowered the glass partition. "John-Michael, is it true? Is Jock leaving me to go work for Tootsie?"

"He was packing up this morning," John-Michael said apologetically. "I thought you knew. You did tell me to fire him and have him clear out today."

"Good heavens, I fire him once a week. He knows not to take it seriously."

"You said you meant it this time. Anyway, he wouldn't have stayed, even if you'd begged him to. He'd made up his mind."

"Well. Thank you, John-Michael, for being honest about it." She raised the glass partition again, then sat back against the leather seat, her face wooden, her hands clasped in her lap.

Sonya didn't know whether to say anything or leave her mother to her thoughts. She didn't know what to say, though, so she remained quiet.

Muffy broke the silence. "How could he leave?"

"Men have their pride."

"I didn't reject him. I just wanted to take things more slowly. Why couldn't he understand that?"

"Mother…might I suggest that Jock leaving could be a good thing?"

"How? Don't tell me you're going to give me a speech about how he's not good enough for me."

"No, of course not. But he was your employee. And that makes a relationship sticky. Why don't you give it a couple of weeks, let him get back on his feet, and then try to see him again—as equals?"

Muffy looked pensive. "I never thought of it like that. But you're right, it did get in the way—the fact I signed his paycheck every week. It was a power struggle, in a way. I had all the power, so he tried to assert his in other ways."

"By digging up your camellias."

Muffy smiled suddenly. "Sonya, you're a genius. That's just what I'll do. I'll give him a couple of weeks. Then that man isn't going to know what hit him." She paused, looking speculatively at Sonya. "Do you think it will help with you and John-Michael? When he's no longer a Patterson employee, I mean."

"I don't know what would help," Sonya grumbled. "Talk about pride."

"I'd fire him today if you thought it would improve your chances."

"Thanks, Mother, but no." That was all Sonya needed—for John-Michael to think she got him fired. Not long ago she'd have snapped up her mother's offer in a heartbeat. Now she couldn't conceive of not having him around, even if their relationship was doomed. He'd be leaving as soon as her wedding date rolled around, or they caught Marvin, whichever came first. Until then, at least she still got to see him.

How pathetic was that?

LATER THAT DAY John-Michael made his decision. His father had made a clean break from the Pattersons, and it was time he did the same. It was no problem for him to move into his rental house a few weeks early. It was empty now, anyway, and the owners would welcome the extra month's rent.

The only thing left to do was tell Muffy—and Sonya.

He waited until after dinner. He spent the afternoon helping Jock move his few belongings into Tootsie's servants quarters, where he would have a private bedroom and bath, and a shared kitchen with the housekeeper, Lucita. Lucita, who'd had the place to herself for a long time, made her resentment clear. But Jock set about charming her, and by that evening she was putting linens on the bed for him and bringing him snacks.

John-Michael left still feeling apprehensive about Jock's new job, but reassured that if anyone could make it work, his father could.

After a fast-food dinner, John-Michael knew he couldn't put it off any longer. He marched into the house and searched until he found Muffy and Sonya in the media room, watching some odious chick-flick tearjerker.

"I need to speak to both of you," he said. And when

Muffy looked alarmed, he hastened to add, "It's nothing bad."

Muffy clicked off the huge, flat-screen TV. "Sit down, John-Michael. There's wine here if you'd like some. Sonya, get him a glass."

Sonya started to rise, but John-Michael halted her. "That's okay, I'm not thirsty. I just…" He sat on the edge of an oversize recliner. This was harder than he thought. "I have some vacation time accumulated, and I'd like to take it."

"Now?" Muffy asked.

"Yes. The house I rented needs a lot of work, and I'd like to get it done before I start my new job."

To his surprise Muffy flashed a quick, secret smile at Sonya. "We'll miss you terribly, you know. Things just won't be the same around here without the McPhee men. But I understand perfectly. I'll speak with June tomorrow morning about cutting your final check."

"Thank you. I appreciate your understanding. I still want to be involved in Marvin's capture, of course. I hope you'll keep me informed when he contacts you again, or if he shows up in person."

Sonya just sat there, looking like a squirrel in the middle of the road, unsure which direction to dive as a car approached. John-Michael knew he had to say something. "Sonya, it's been a pleasure looking after you."

"Don't be a fat liar," she said. "I've been terrible, and you've hated every minute of it."

"Not every minute." He took her cold hand, squeezed it.

She snatched it back. "Coward."

"Sonya!" Muffy objected. "Manners."

"Well, he is a coward. He can't just look me in the eye and say, 'Sonya, I'm not interested in you.' He has to create some drama about how we're all wrong for each other because I'm rich and he's not. I just want some honesty from him."

John-Michael recoiled. He wasn't prepared to discuss this in front of Muffy. Hell, he wasn't prepared to discuss it at all. How much had Sonya told her mother?

Muffy didn't look shocked. In fact, she looked amused. "By all means, John-Mikey," she said, trotting out the nickname she used only in times of great emotion or great irritation. "My daughter wants to know how you feel about her. Are you interested? Or did you just sleep with her because she was available?"

John-Michael would have gladly suffered through an epileptic seizure right about now if it could have extricated him from this…this interrogation. "I…I have a great deal of respect and admiration—" he began, but both women interrupted.

"Oh, please!" they said in unison.

"How lame," Muffy added. "John-Michael, I thought better of you."

"All right, fine. You want honesty, you'll get it. I do have feelings for Sonya. I might even go so far as to say that I've fallen in love with her. But deep inside, I know we could not be compatible in the long run. I'm choosing to remove myself rather than set us both up for a hell of a heartache."

"And I repeat," Sonya said. "You're a coward. If you really loved me, you'd take a chance."

John-Michael didn't think he would get a better exit line. He got out of there before he could change his mind.

Sonya and Muffy stared at each other for a full minute after he'd gone.

"He loves you," Muffy said.

"How can he just walk out if he loves me?"

"I've been asking myself the same question all day. But I believe Jock does love me. And John-Michael loves you. Let's give them a little time to figure out they're better off with us than without us." She flicked the TV back on and they resumed watching *Steel Magnolias.* By the time it was over, they'd emptied two full boxes of tissues.

Chapter Twelve

As the weeks passed and the wedding date grew closer, Sonya came very close to losing her nerve. Marvin had called her two more times. Both conversations were short, but he had reiterated that he would be there for the ceremony.

After the first of those calls, she had immediately dialed John-Michael's cell number, elated that she had a reason to call him. He'd told her to keep him informed, after all. But she'd only reached his voice mail and had ended up leaving a lame message. He had called back, reached *her* voice mail, and assured her he was looking into her phone records to see if he could get a fix on Marvin's location. But she didn't hear from him after that, so she assumed he wasn't successful.

After the second call from Marvin, she called the FBI, figuring they might be interested that she had heard from him. But the guy she talked to at the Houston Field Office didn't seem very interested in staking out her wedding. He had bigger fish to fry—serial killers, bank robbers, child molesters. Marvin's case had belonged to Heath. When he left the FBI, much of the impetus to catch Marvin had gone with him, it seemed.

She needed a plan, she decided. She could not count on John-Michael to be there for her. And even if he kept his word and showed up when she needed him to catch Marvin, he was just one man. Marvin had escaped when whole hoards of law enforcement people were after him. One man—even John-Michael—might not be able to take Marvin into custody.

Christmas passed with no word from Marvin, the FBI, or John-Michael. When a large package arrived for Sonya two days after Christmas, she didn't open it right away, assuming it was another gift from her mother, who'd gone hog-wild with her mail-order catalogs this year. But after it sat for a couple of days in the foyer, she got curious.

When she saw that the package was from Delta Optics, she realized it was the gift she'd ordered weeks ago for John-Michael. She'd once felt delicious anticipation at the thought of giving it to him, but now she just felt sad.

She would hire a messenger to deliver it to his new home, she decided, along with a friendly but impersonal note of explanation. But somehow, she never actually got around to calling the messenger service and writing the note.

Sonya had long ago convinced her maid of honor, Cissy Trask-Burnside, to cancel the "couples shower" she'd had planned for December. But Cissy, determined to have some kind of party, threw a New Year's Eve bash and told everyone who was coming that they could bring shower gifts for Sonya.

Sonya couldn't avoid attending the party without causing a major flack. The society reporter, Leslie Frazier, was there, which necessitated Sonya again doing some fast talking about why her fiancé was never around.

She trotted out the very excuses Marvin had given her—he was stuck in a maze of bureaucratic red tape and could not leave Beijing until he'd straightened it all out. The lies just poured out of Sonya—she had a real talent for deception, she realized somewhat uncomfortably—and everyone took them at face value.

After Leslie left, conversation turned to other gossip—whose husband was cheating, who had committed a fashion faux pas. Sonya was horribly bored, and she longed for her other friends, Brenna and Cindy. The three of them used to talk long into the night about all kinds of things—history and philosophy, movies and books, and of course men and sex. Not that they were intellectuals or anything, but at least their topics of interest had been a bit broader than whose husband had bought her a new car, and what she had given in return.

Sonya frankly couldn't understand why she'd remained friends with Cissy for so long when all they had in common these days was that they'd once belonged to the same sorority.

Her two other bridesmaids were in attendance. One of them got drunk, tripped over the front steps on her way out, and had to make a trip to the emergency room with a broken ankle. The other bridesmaid confessed to Sonya that her sister-in-law had decided to get married the same weekend as Sonya—in Aruba. "But I gave you my word," she said with pompous loyalty.

Sonya couldn't possibly ask Krystal to give up a real wedding in Aruba for a fake one in Houston. She insisted that Krystal make plans for Aruba. "I'll miss you terribly, but your own family is more important. I can find someone to fill in."

"But the dress—"

"I can have it altered. It'll be fine."

Anyway, she had a plan.

At five minutes to midnight, she dialed Brenna's cell number. "Sonya! Where are you?"

"A boring party." Sonya was hiding in a linen cupboard, the only place quiet and private enough. "Listen, I need your help. Do you want to be a bridesmaid?"

"Don't you already have bridesmaids?"

"They're dropping like flies. Plus, I'd just as soon have real friends here with me. January 8. Can you be here? And your hunky fiancé, too." Heath and Brenna had recently announced their engagement.

"Aren't you carrying this fake wedding thing a bit far?"

"I'm absolutely convinced Marvin will show up. The prospect of getting his hands on Mother's money is just too tempting. But once he's here, I'll need help with the takedown."

"What about Mr. Muscle-Man Bodyguard?"

Sonya's throat went tight at the reminder. "I can't really count on him. And even if I could, it'll take more than one person. I need you, and more importantly, I need Heath. I'm going to ask Cindy and Luke, too."

"I'm in," Brenna said. "And I'm sure Heath will want to be there, too. I'll let you talk to Cindy, she's right here."

"She is? Oh, hi, Cindy! I hate that y'all are celebrating without me." Sonya had been invited to the annual New Year's bash thrown by Brenna's parents, but she'd felt obligated to attend Cissy's party, since it was sort of in her honor.

"We wish you were here, too," Cindy said. Without hesitation, Cindy agreed to be in the wedding. "Will we have to wear really embarrassing, frou-frou pink dresses?"

"Forest-green velvet monstrosities," Sonya confirmed. "I'll have yours Fed-Exed to you so you can have it fitted."

"Oh…oh, the ball is dropping. Happy New Year!"

Sonya could hear the cheering coming from the great room in Cissy's house, as well as over the phone. She assumed by the fumbling and strange noises that Cindy's husband was kissing the daylights out of her, and her heart felt heavy.

She and John-Michael could be locking lips this very minute if he weren't such a fool. She'd been waiting, giving him time and space as Muffy had suggested, and nothing had happened.

Muffy, however, was having better luck. She had called Jock, ostensibly to get his advice about an ailing houseplant. Surprised by her conciliatory tone, he'd wound up asking to meet her for coffee, to discuss her houseplant problem in detail. He had picked her up in his little Volvo station wagon, washed and waxed for the occasion. Afterward, they'd gone to a movie. Then he'd brought her home, walked her to the door, kissed her on the cheek, then had said something that had left Muffy giggling. Sonya had been watching out a window.

Tonight they were at some fancy shindig at a hotel. Sonya had asked Muffy how she would handle it if the press got wind of the fact she was dating her former gardener, but Muffy had said she was sick to death of worrying about what people thought, and that was that.

"Are you still there?" Cindy asked breathlessly.

"If I weren't engaged, I'd be making out with one of the cute bartenders right now," Sonya said glumly.

"Oh, no. You sound so sad."

"I just wish it was all over."

"Maybe by next weekend, we'll have reason to celebrate. Picture Marvin behind bars."

"With a mean cellmate named Snake."

SONYA'S WEDDING WAS in three days. John-Michael tried not to think about it as he drove his squad car, his new partner, Greg Sandusky, in the passenger seat. The Harris County Sheriff's Department had been only too happy to move up his start date. So now he had his crisp khaki uniform, his gun, his badge. It was everything he'd been looking forward to all these years.

He was free of the Pattersons, and so was his father. He had his own place, which he'd been working on every evening, scrubbing and painting, trimming the overgrown shrubs, putting in new light fixtures. He had his own two-car garage for his car and his motorcycle and his tools. Once he clocked out, he was on his own time, no longer at Muffy's or Sonya's beck and call.

He should have been in heaven. Instead, he was miserable. During work, he could forget about Sonya for a little while. Today, for example, he'd used his negotiating skills—honed from many, many incidents with his father—to calm a domestic disturbance before it got violent. The work was interesting and satisfying.

But the moment John-Michael clocked out and got into his own car, all he could think about was how much he missed Sonya. He tried to tell himself it was only natural. He'd spent so much time with her, that to be suddenly without her was going to take some adjustment.

But he knew it was more than that. He'd fallen in love with the darn woman. He imagined her everywhere, working side by side with him in the kitchen to fix dinner, cozying next to him in the evenings to read, or in bed with him, losing themselves in the mind-blowing sex he remembered way too vividly.

But he doubted Sonya's fantasies were in line with his. If she visualized them together at all, she probably saw him moving into the big house with her, sharing dinner every night at that football-field-size dining table, eating the delicious meals Mattie and Eric prepared, socializing with her tedious highbrow friends and enduring their disapproval.

Much as he wanted to be with her, he couldn't partake in that life. He wasn't cut out to be one of the idle rich. Even if he worked, his paycheck would be superfluous, a joke. Maybe it was his foolish pride overruling his common sense, but he wasn't going to turn into his father, forever craving something with Sonya he couldn't have.

He was just going to have to get over her.

Of course, there was the wedding to endure. He'd had a brief conversation with Muffy yesterday—Sonya hadn't wanted to talk to him. Muffy had coolly informed him that Marvin was scheduled to arrive at ten a.m. at Houston Intercontinental Airport the morning of January 8. Marvin had given Sonya the airline and flight number, arriving from Hong Kong.

As a fully sworn law enforcement officer, John-Michael found that he had a bit more clout than he had as a bodyguard—and more resources. With the FBI's cooperation and assistance, he'd been able to check the flight's passenger list. Marvin's name did not appear, though he might be traveling under one of his many aliases.

This might be a test, John-Michael theorized. Marvin might stake out his supposed arrival gate to see what kind of greeting awaited him, whether there were any law enforcement types ready to nab him. If not, he could figure Sonya was really on the level, that she didn't believe he had ripped her off, or had conveniently forgotten because she wanted to marry him so badly.

John-Michael intended to watch the gate—though he would be well-hidden. Greg Sandusky had agreed to help him. The airline had been faxed Marvin's photo and would be able to let them know ahead of time if he was on the plane, though even if they said he wasn't, John-Michael would be there. Marvin's disguises were pretty good.

He felt some sense of anticipation that Marvin might finally be captured. But he hoped to have it all neatly tied up before the wedding. He didn't think he could stand to see Sonya in that white gown again, forever the princess, so totally out of his league.

As he turned down his street, he saw something that made him prickle with apprehension. His father's station wagon was parked in front of his house. Had he lost his job already?

He pulled into the garage, then walked around to the front porch, where Jock sat on the steps, chin in hand.

"Dad?"

Jock popped to his feet. "John-Michael. God Almighty, look at you in that uniform! If that ain't a sight. I'm really proud of you, son. I know this is something you've wanted for a long time."

"I…um, thanks, Dad." He shook his father's proffered hand, then glanced at Jock's Volvo. It was packed to the gills.

"I've left Tootsie's. I guess you figured that out."

"What happened?" John-Michael wasn't sure he wanted to know. If Jock had gotten drunk and done something—

"It's nothing like you're thinking. It's just that Tootsie is as horrible as we've always heard she was. What a dictator! She demanded the impossible, and when I delivered, it wasn't good enough. This past month, I've gained a whole new appreciation for Muffy Patterson as an employer."

"Did you quit?"

"Yes, I did."

Well, that was a relief. No one would fault Jock for resigning as Tootsie's gardener. Everyone knew she couldn't keep household help. "Do you think Muffy would take you back?"

At the mention of Muffy's name, Jock smiled, but at the same time he shook his head. "No, I'm not going back there, either. I'm a hot commodity!" he said proudly. "When I resigned, of course Tootsie got on the phone to all of her friends and complained about it. Within a half hour I had three job offers."

"Great, Dad! Which one are you taking?"

"None of them," he said, looking pleased with himself. "I've decided to go into business for myself. I'll start small, doing some landscaping and garden design, and flower arrangements for parties and such. But eventually, I'd like to have my own greenhouse. I could be like that swishy guy down in Sugarland, the one Sonya got her wedding flowers from."

John-Michael was floored. He'd never seen his father so excited about anything. Jock knew nothing about running a business. He probably had no idea the headaches he was in for—the bookkeeping, the paperwork that went with paying employees, the taxes, billing and collecting. But John-Michael wasn't about to rain on Jock's parade. If he started small and learned as he went, it might just work.

"I think that's great, Dad. I'll help you if I can." He nodded toward the station wagon. "I take it you need a place to live."

"Just until I find my own place. I need to do some looking around, figure out the best location. A couple, maybe three weeks. I've got a lot of money saved."

"I'll help you unload the car."

"SO, HOW IS IT living here?" Jock asked a couple of hours later. John-Michael was broiling them some pork chops while his father cut up carrots to zap in the microwave.

"It's a quiet neighborhood," John-Michael said. "It's not too far from where I work, and it's near the water. So far it's okay."

"I don't mean that. I mean, how does it feel, being away from the Pattersons? Is it as good as you thought it would be?"

"In some ways, yes."

"Don't you miss her?"

John-Michael didn't have to ask who "her" was. "Of course I do. Do you miss Muffy?"

"Well, it's kind of hard to miss someone when you're seeing them every night." Jock let this little bombshell drop just as John-Michael was transferring a pork chop from broiler to plate, and he jerked so hard in surprise that the chop flew off the fork and landed with a splat on the kitchen counter.

"What did you say?"

"Muffy and I are dating. It seems I misunderstood what she was trying to tell me the night everything hit the fan. She wasn't ashamed of me. She just didn't want to move as fast as I did."

"You and Muffy are *dating?*" John-Michael hadn't gotten past the first sentence.

"Moving away from the Patterson estate was the smartest thing I ever could have done. I wish I'd done it twenty years ago. Instead I let myself pine away for something I couldn't have, drank myself into a stupor when the pain of seeing her and not being able to have her got to be too much. As if me being drunk gave her any reason to change her mind. If I had left back then, made something of myself—well, no sense looking back. But maybe I'm not too old to make something of myself now. And with the moral support of Muffy, who knows how far I'll go?

"You and Muffy are *dating?*" He wasn't usually slow on the uptake, but this was way beyond anything he could have imagined.

"We're dating the way we couldn't when we were kids. We go to the movies, out for hamburgers—well, baked chicken sandwiches in Muffy's case, since she's not allowed to eat hamburgers. We even played miniature golf, just about froze our tushies off!"

John-Michael abandoned the stove and sank into a chair. He was in shock.

"You want to know the best part?" Jock asked.

"I'm not sure."

"She said she doesn't care who knows about us. That anyone who faults her for dating her former gardener is a snob, and she doesn't want to be friends with them anyway. On New Year's Eve, we'd planned to go to one of those dreary AA bashes, but at the last minute we went to this party at a fancy hotel. Muffy said someone gave her the tickets, although I think she might have bought them because she knew it was a little beyond my budget. Anyway, we ran into a lot of her friends there, and she introduced me as her date. Some of them gave us queer looks, but some of them treated me just fine. It was amazing."

John-Michael thought about his father, surrounded by all that drinking, and he had to ask. "Did you stay sober?"

"Oh, sure. Ginger ale all the way. Wasn't even tempted. I was high on Muffy."

John-Michael struggled to adjust his thinking. Was it possible Jock and Muffy could make things work after all these years, overlook the monumental differences in their backgrounds and financial status?

"I'm telling you all this not to brag," Jock said, "but to make it clear that I was wrong before. Yes, I needed to get away from being the Patterson gardener, but I didn't need to escape from Muffy. All I needed was to feel worthy of her. She'll always be richer than me, more educated, more refined. But I can still be her equal. And that's what matters."

"I'm happy for you, Dad. And I really hope it works out. I've always liked Muffy. I've always believed she had a good heart."

"And what about Sonya?"

John-Michael's defensive walls sprang up. "What about her?"

"How do you feel about her?"

"It doesn't matter how I feel about her," John-Michael said carefully. "She's getting married in a couple of days."

"Don't be daft. Muffy told me the wedding's a sham to catch that unholy con artist."

All right, so John-Michael wasn't going to extricate himself from this conversation with that ploy. How could he answer?

"You don't have to say anything, I see it in your face. You're crazy in love with the girl. Well, I happen to know for a fact she's crazy in love with you. I'm not supposed to say anything, but I'm not going to stand around and watch you make all the same stupid mistakes Muffy and I did. If you love her, do something about it."

John-Michael couldn't say what he really wanted to—that a union between the heiress and the gardener's son was doomed. He would be dooming Jock's own romance, too, and he couldn't do that, not when his father was so excited, so upbeat and optimistic.

John-Michael asked a question instead. "What are Muffy's feelings on the subject?"

"Muffy wants her daughter to be happy. She spent the last ten years shopping for the perfect husband for Sonya, driving away every single man who came along because he didn't meet her standards. Then she met Marvin, and she thought he was perfect. And look how wrong she was. She sees that now. And she has vowed to stay out of Sonya's love life from now on."

"So she thinks I would be a disastrous choice for Sonya, but she's keeping her mouth shut."

"On the contrary. She thinks you would make a fine son-in-law. But other than telling Sonya to follow her heart, she's staying out of it. 'Course, that doesn't mean *I* have to stay out of it."

So Muffy wouldn't object. That was one obstacle out

of the way. John-Michael was shocked by the direction his thoughts were taking.

"Take a chance," Jock said in a soft voice. "If it doesn't work out, it'll hurt like hell and then you'll go on. But if you do nothing, you'll tear your life apart with regret, condemn yourself to a purgatory of your own making—halfway between heaven and hell. Trust me, you'll regret never trying, forever."

"So you're actually in this country?" Sonya asked, trying to sound excited. It was 8 a.m. the day of her wedding, and Marvin had called her on her cell. She'd been afraid he would pull something like this. Her dreams of seeing him apprehended at the airport when the flight from Hong Kong arrived dissipated like the steam from her coffee cup.

Brenna, Heath, Cindy and Luke were seated at the breakfast table with her, enjoying Matilda's buckwheat pancakes and fresh fruit, when the phone had rung. They all went silent when they realized who was on the other end of Sonya's call, watching her intently.

"I'm actually at Dulles," he said. "God, it's good to be on American soil again. I'm going to get the first flight I can find to Houston. But the weather is a bit iffy. There was a storm last night, lots of flights backed up. But if I have to charter a plane, I'll get there in time, I swear it."

"I know you will, darling. I have complete faith in you." She almost choked on the words, then disconnected.

"Wow," Brenna said. "You're a lot better at lying to Marvin than I was."

"No kidding," Heath said, earning an elbow in the ribs from his fiancée for his trouble. "We need to update John-Michael. It's pointless now to try to catch him at the airport."

Heath had left the FBI and started his own private investigation firm, but he had the most experience dealing with desperate criminals, so he'd been voted the leader of Operation Nab Marvin. His cell phone rang almost immediately. Sonya knew who it would be. She couldn't watch, couldn't listen. John-Michael would have been contacted by her cell phone company, which had her number flagged.

Sonya got up and took her plate to the sink so no one could see her face.

"Yes, that was Marvin," Heath said into his phone. "I was about to call—he's in Houston?"

Now Sonya had to listen. Marvin was right there in their city, so close.

"Uh-huh. Okay. We're on it." Heath hung up. "Marvin is downtown. John-Michael has it narrowed down to a few blocks, based on the cell tower his signal came from. There are several hotels in the area. We're going to check them out, see if he might be staying in one of them."

"I want to come," Sonya said automatically.

"If he sees you, he'll know the jig is up and run," Heath said reasonably.

"But he knows you, too," Sonya argued. Heath had been face-to-face with Marvin in New York, before he'd slithered out of Heath's grasp.

Heath donned a baseball cap, a pair of black-framed

glasses, a stick-on mustache and a set of fake front teeth, one of them gold.

Brenna buried her face in her hands. "Oh, my gosh, this is so embarrassing. He's taking this private investigator thing too seriously."

But the disguise was effective.

Heath and Luke took off, leaving the women alone.

"All right, what gives?" Brenna asked. "Every time John-Michael McPhee's name is mentioned, you get this pained look on your face like someone just stabbed you in the heart."

"Yeah, you're holding out on us," Cindy added. "We've told you every gory detail of our love lives."

This was the first time Sonya had been alone with her two girlfriends since they'd arrived yesterday. She'd actually been dying to unload on them. "John-Michael McPhee is a complete jerk, unworthy of my angst. He slept with me and immediately dumped me. I mean, okay, I'm the one who seduced him, sort of, but he could have refused, knowing I was making an utter fool of myself."

"He dumped you?" Cindy said, outraged. "Right after sex?"

"We were still in bed," Sonya confirmed.

Brenna made a fist. "Never mind Marvin. Just let John-Michael McPhee show his face around here. I'll slap him up the side of the head."

"Hold on," Cindy said. "Sonya, did he say, 'I don't want to be with you'? In so many words?"

Sonya nodded. "He made it sound like he's doing me a favor by removing himself from my life, like I'm too good for him or he's too bad for me or—" She stopped, took a few gulps of orange juice before she started crying again. She set the glass down with a clunk and looked at her watch. "I don't need to be thinking about this now. I have to get dressed for my stupid hair appointment, so I can show up for a stupid wedding and make an idiot of myself very publicly."

"Making a fool of yourself has an upside," Brenna said. "My jewelry orders tripled after the *Morning News* ran that story about me diving into a mountain of shrimp and breaking off the ice-Diana's arm. Couldn't get much more foolish than that."

"Everybody in my hometown knew what a fool I was," Cindy chimed in. "But they all rallied around me when I needed them. The true friends will understand. And the others—who cares about them?"

Sonya got up, walked around the table and hugged each of her friends in turn. "I am so glad you two are here. I wouldn't be able to survive this without you to put things in perspective. I just never imagined we would have to take it this far."

"You're really brave," Cindy said. "And your mom is great, paying for a phony wedding just so we can have our vengeance."

"The reception will be a big victory party if our plan works."

"And a big pity party if it doesn't," said Brenna. "But I'm with you all the way."

Chapter Thirteen

John-Michael walked up to the glossy marble check-in desk at the Blue Heron Hotel, the sixth he'd approached in the past two hours. He introduced himself, showed the clerk his shiny new Harris County Sheriff's Department badge, and made his requests. Though he wore no uniform and this was not an official investigation and he had no warrant, the various clerks had been incredibly cooperative.

This one was no exception. She checked her computer. "No, I'm sorry, there's no one by the name of Marvin Carter registered," the young woman said.

John-Michael then showed her the pictures he'd managed to accumulate of Marvin in various guises— dark hair, blond, mustache, clean-shaven, glasses, no glasses.

"Wait, that guy does look familiar," she said thoughtfully. "I didn't check him in, but maybe someone else remembers something." She consulted with the other clerks on duty, then the assistant manager. Finally one cocky young man came forward. "I checked that guy in a couple of days ago. Swenson was the last name. Is he a dangerous fugitive or something?"

"I'd just like to speak to him, if I could."

The manager stepped forward. "We can't give you his room number for privacy reasons," she said sternly. "But we can connect you via the house phone."

No, that wouldn't do. Any warning at all, and Marvin would be scurrying down some fire escape or service elevator, and they would have lost yet another chance to catch him. "Thanks, but no." He stepped away from the desk and into the luxurious lobby, where he called the other members of his arrest party, who were canvassing other hotels, restaurants and office buildings in the area.

"We'll have to get a warrant," Heath said. "McPhee, you're the only one with jurisdiction here. You know any friendly judges?"

"Hell, no! I just started this job two weeks ago."

"Then we'll have to do this the hard way."

As the plan unfolded, Luke Rheems waited in the hotel lobby and watched in case Marvin happened to walk through. John-Michael made a few phone calls, then went with Heath to the county courthouse to cajole a judge into issuing a court order, instructing the hotel to cough up "Mr. Swenson's" room number. It took some convincing, too, and a half-dozen phone calls before the judge was convinced of exactly how urgent the need was to apprehend Carter.

By the time they returned to the Blue Heron, it was two o'clock—an hour before the wedding was scheduled to begin. They presented the court order, got Marvin's room number. The head of security accompanied them up to the eighth floor.

They made a hasty plan, drew their weapons, stuck the pass key in the door and pushed it open.

"Police!" the three of them shouted at the same time as they burst into the room. The empty room.

The disappointment hit John-Michael like a sucker-punch to the jaw, but he tried not to let it show. He and the others gave the room a hasty search and found receipts for a tuxedo rental and a carnation boutonnière.

"We'll catch up with him at the church," Heath said as they brushed past the bewildered manager standing in the hall.

John-Michael moved at a dead run for his car, parked on the next block. Sure, the church was only thirty minutes away—if the traffic cooperated. But if they ran into one of Houston's ubiquitous traffic jams, all bets were off.

The thought of that monster within a hundred feet of Sonya made him sick to his stomach. During a brief phone conversation with Muffy earlier this morning, he'd assured her they would do everything they could to arrest Marvin before the wedding started.

It was as he feared—Interstate 110 was blocked solid due to an accident, according to his police scanner. He took the surface streets. He could still get there in time. Unfortunately, a glance in his rearview mirror told him Heath and Luke weren't behind him. Unfamiliar with Houston's traffic as they were, they wouldn't know the best route. But he couldn't wait for them.

He had to get to Sonya.

IN THE BRIDE'S ROOM at St. Eustace Episcopal Church, Sonya paced and chewed on one of her acrylic nails until all the polish was off. Cindy and Brenna, dressed in the lush green velvet dresses, tried to calm her down, while Cissy Trask-Burnside, her matron of honor, sat in a corner in complete shock. They'd finally had to tell her what was going on, and ever since, she'd looked as if she wanted to escape this sordid little party and hop the first plane for the Bahamas.

"They'll catch him this time," Cindy said. "Last time Heath called, he said they had Marvin cornered in a hotel room."

"He could still escape," Sonya said. "I could see him going out a window and jumping into an awning, or getting smuggled out on a housekeeping cart by some maid he seduced."

Brenna's phone rang. Heath had been keeping her updated all day. She grabbed it. "Heath? Do you have him?"

Sonya watched Brenna's face as she listened. Brenna frowned. "Oh, no. Oh, *no!*"

"What?" Sonya and Cindy said together.

"When they went to his room, he was gone," Brenna said. "They're absolutely positive he's headed here, planning to get married."

"That means we can still catch him," Sonya said hopefully.

"But here's the worst part. Heath and Luke are stuck in traffic. A complete log jam on the freeway."

"Where's John-Michael?" Sonya asked.

"They don't know. They lost sight of him."

"He should be here soon—he avoided the worst of the traffic. But if he doesn't make it in time, Heath said we should continue with the wedding." Brenna looked uncomfortable as she added, "You can always have the marriage annulled."

Sonya felt panicky at the thought. "All right, girls, it's up to us," she said resolutely. "We can't count on any of the guys to get here in time. So here's what we'll do. We'll wait as long as can—right up to before Father Jewell declares us husband and wife. And if the real lawmen haven't arrived by then, we jump Marvin, tackle him to the ground, and sit on him until help arrives."

"You're insane, all of you," said Cissy, who had never really grasped the true situation. "I want no part in this."

"Then stay out of the way," Sonya said, wondering why she'd never noticed before how dense Cissy was.

Just then, the bride's room door flew open and in strolled Marvin Carter, looking slicker than Brylcreem in a tuxedo. He had shadows under his eyes Sonya didn't remember from before, and he appeared as if he might have lost a bit of weight. But otherwise he was perfectly groomed, devastatingly handsome—even with brown hair and a goatee.

Cindy and Brenna turned quickly and pulled the heavy veils from their headpieces over their faces. Mrs. Kim had been persuaded to add the veils at the last minute.

"Darling!" Marvin said breathlessly as he swept Sonya into his arms. "At last, at last, I'm here. It's been a nightmare."

Oh, I'll just bet. "Marvin, sweetheart," Sonya said, hoping he wouldn't detect the revulsion in her voice. How in the world had she ever fancied she was in love with this horrible man? She hugged him, avoiding the kiss he attempted to give her. "My lipstick."

Muffy appeared at the doorway, visibly vibrating with tension. "Sonya? Darling? It's three o'clock. Time to get started." Her voice was tight with strain.

The last thing Sonya wanted to do was stress out her mother. "Mother, it's all fine," she said. "The *plans* are in place, everything's perfect. Now all we have to do is let the wedding unfold."

Muffy looked doubtful, but she laid a hand on Marvin's forearm. "It's so wonderful to see you, Marvin. We were so worried. Go to the front of the church, now, and wait for your bride."

"My pleasure," he said with an oily smile to all of them.

As soon as he departed, Muffy demanded, "Where's John-Michael? And the other fellows?"

"On their way," Sonya said. "We have to just carry on like normal until they arrive. I don't think Marvin suspects a thing."

From the church vestibule, Sonya watched as an usher showed her mother to her seat at the front of the church. Then her two bridesmaids walked as slowly as they dared down the aisle and took up their places near the front, where Father Jewell, the ancient priest, stood in his fancy vestments awaiting to officiate the marriage ceremony.

There were no groomsmen. Marvin hadn't asked anyone to stand up for him. If the wedding party appeared a bit lopsided, everyone pretended they didn't notice. Cissy walked down the aisle, glorying in the attention, poor clueless thing.

The church was beautiful. The flowers were perfect. Muffy had done an outstanding job.

Sonya clutched the breathtaking bouquet Jock had made for her. He had such a talent. Then the music she'd chosen for her march down the aisle began. She took Jock's arm—she'd asked him to give her away, and he'd been honored, even at the last minute. He cut a handsome figure in his sober, dark-gray suit.

"What's happening?" he whispered.

"We're waiting for the cavalry to arrive," Sonya whispered back. She hadn't expected to feel such high emotion when faced with the culmination of all her and her mother's carefully laid plans. It was a beautiful wedding—the colors, the candles, the music and her princess-bride dress. She knew she would never achieve such matrimonial perfection again. This was it. This was the only fancy wedding she would ever have.

And John-Michael should have been the groom she was marrying. As infuriating as the man was, as much as he'd hurt her, she still loved him. She would always love him, she supposed. Which meant she was doomed to spend the rest of her life alone. Even if she found another man to make her a decent husband, even a man she was genuinely fond of, she couldn't expect him to marry her when her heart remained with John-Michael.

Marvin stood at the front of the church, his smile beatific. She was sure everyone there was sighing at his eagerness, thinking how romantic it was that he'd managed to escape from the clutches of repressive government officials in China to make his own wedding in the nick of time.

"Be ready for anything," she whispered to Jock as she kissed his cheek and he put her hand into Marvin's.

JOHN-MICHAEL WAS STOPPED by two rent-a-cops just outside the church—security Muffy had hired to keep out reporters and other riff-raff. They checked his name against a list and let him pass. He slipped in through a door at the back of the church. Judging from the hush, the ceremony had already begun, though it was only seven minutes after three.

At least he'd had the presence of mind to put a jacket and tie into his car before his trip downtown, just in case he ran short of time. Tying his tie, he walked up the side aisle to a pew very close to the front of the church. The elderly minister was droning on and on about the sanctity of marriage.

John-Michael looked around, hoping Heath and Luke would appear so he wouldn't have to do this bust on his own. Thus far in his short law enforcement career, he'd made two arrests. One had been for public intoxication, and one was some poor schmo with a bench warrant for about two dozen parking tickets. Neither had resisted.

Marvin Carter would resist. Knowing how slippery the guy was, John-Michael wasn't thrilled to do this on his own. But he would—and soon, if the rest of his team didn't show up.

He tried not to look at Sonya. But he couldn't help it. God, she was beautiful, her face pale, her golden hair gleaming in its elaborate twists and curls. His heart ached, he wanted to touch her so badly, reassure her that he *would* come to her rescue.

He focused instead on Marvin, standing tall and proud beside his bride, thinking he had it made. The Patterson fortune, so close, almost in his hands.

The couple said their vows in shaking voices, and still no Heath and Luke. This was it, then. John-Michael stood, walked around the pew to the front, making his way unobtrusively toward the groom.

"If anyone knows why these two should not be joined in holy matrimony, let him speak now or forever—"

"I object," John-Michael said.

Marvin tensed and looked as if he could flee any moment.

"I'm in love with the bride," John-Michael declared passionately.

"Who the hell are you?" Marvin demanded.

"Don't you remember?" Sonya asked. "You met him many times. He was my bodyguard, John-Michael McPhee." And she was smiling.

Marvin laughed harshly. "Oh, that's rich, not to mention pathetic, getting a crush on your boss."

Sonya gave Marvin a scornful look. "Oh, shut up, you repulsive slime-bucket!" The congregation gasped. She stepped in front of Marvin and took John-Michael's hand. "John-Michael, do you mean it? Or is this just a stalling tactic?"

John-Michael had intended to object on the basis that the groom was a wanted felon and thus not a fit husband. Instead, his true feelings had poured out of him with no conscious decision on his part—and he hadn't really been prepared for the consequences.

"Yes, I do mean it," he said. "I tried to tell myself you'd be better off without me mucking up your high-society life, that you would be happier marrying one of your own class. But then I saw you here, about to marry *him*—"

"Excuse me," said the priest. "Is there a problem?"

But Sonya acted as if she couldn't even hear him. "I would give away everything to charity if I thought it would make a difference. I love you, John-Michael. I've loved you since I was a little girl, and you worked so hard to cheer me up after my father died."

"You're not going to marry Marvin or anyone else but me."

"No, I'm not."

They kissed, a sweet, almost chaste kiss, and everyone in the church applauded.

"Marvin!" someone cried out. "He's getting away!"

MARVIN SHOULD HAVE KNOWN it was too good to be true. He'd almost had the ring on his finger. A guarantee of a life of luxury and ease had been within his grasp. And then that musclebound Romeo had ruined everything!

Marvin would have punched the guy in the nose—except the bodyguard was bigger and stronger than Marvin, and Marvin probably would not have come out on top in a physical confrontation.

No, the best thing for him to do now was disappear, before his past caught up with him.

He made it to a side exit. He opened the door, smelling freedom. He hadn't wanted to be married anyway, he told himself. He might have ended up rich, but he'd have been in prison, with Sonya and her mother as the wardens. Better he should return to Europe, lie low for a while longer. He had a lovely Swedish masseuse waiting for him in a hotel room in Paris.

He started to step outside into the bright winter sun when he was met by two large men with grim faces. As recognition dawned, he realized he was in more trouble than he thought. It was that hayseed sheriff from the Podunk town where Cindy lived. And the FBI agent from New York!

They reached out to grab Marvin, but he ducked, turned and ran back into the church, only to run headlong into a sea of angry faces—the bride, for one. Two blond bridesmaids—again, recognition dawned. Cindy and Brenna! He'd been had.

At the front of the pack was the bodyguard with a pair of handcuffs in one hand.

No way out of this except to fight his way out. He aimed a punch square for the bodyguard's face.

SONYA SAW THE PUNCH coming at John-Michael. Rather than just staying out of the way, which would have been the smart thing to do, Sonya jumped forward and tried to block the punch. She succeeded in blocking it—with her face. The punch wasn't hard enough to break anything, just enough to make her eyes water.

Suddenly all the pain and stress and outrage of the past few months burbled to the surface. Sonya had heard of people seeing red, but now she discovered it was literally true. She saw Marvin's face through a haze of red—and he looked at least as surprised as she felt.

She didn't wait for him to apologize. Without conscious thought, her hand clenched into a fist, she drew her arm back, and she punched Marvin in his handsome, aristocratic face.

His eyes crossed like a cartoon character's. He staggered back, then crumpled into a heap on the plush maroon carpet runner.

"Man, did that feel good," Sonya said with a triumphant smile as months of stress drained from her body.

Her two bridesmaids cheered and clapped. Then they pounced as one on Marvin's inert form. Cindy yanked a long ribbon from her bouquet, pulled Marvin's hands behind them, and bound them with the red satin. Brenna ripped a length of chiffon from her headpiece and wound it around Marvin's ankles, tying it in knot after knot.

"Er, I have handcuffs," John-Michael said.

"I'm not taking any chances," Brenna said. "You better put leg irons and a ball and chain on him if you want to prevent him from escaping."

Heath and Luke pushed through the crowd.

"It's about time," John-Michael grumbled.

Luke grinned. "Looks like we weren't needed, anyway."

Heath examined the bindings around Marvin's wrists and ankles. "Our own blushing brides took matters into their own hands."

Luke and Heath grasped Marvin by his arms and hauled him to his feet. He was conscious but dazed. "You set me up," he sputtered to Sonya. "This was a trap!"

"Oh, poor baby," Sonya said. "Am I supposed to feel pity? I'm going to make sure you spend the rest of your life making license plates."

He stared at her in disbelief. "And to think, I was actually in love with you."

"You don't know what love is," Sonya replied, and there was sadness in her voice, rather than rancor. She took John-Michael's hand in hers. "Love is putting the other person first, thinking about their needs before your own." She gave John-Michael a meaningful look. "I'm lucky. I know what it is to be loved—by my friends, my family and John-Michael. I hope you find that someday, Marvin, and that you properly appreciate it when you do."

He looked somewhat bewildered by her speech as Heath and Luke literally carried him down the center aisle of the cathedral-like church and out the massive double doors. They left his feet bound, unwilling to take any chances.

John-Michael turned to Sonya. "Sweetheart, you're bleeding."

"Here," Muffy said as she handed John-Michael a handkerchief. He used it to gently wipe under Sonya's nose.

"Ugh. I've bled on my beautiful dress." She hadn't felt much pain when adrenaline had been coursing through her veins. But now that it was all over, her nose hurt and the hand she'd used to punch Marvin throbbed with pain. She looked at her red, swollen fingers and wondered idly if she'd broken anything.

And then she remembered. John-Michael had said he loved her and wanted to marry her. And she'd agreed!

The ancient priest came tottering up to them. "Are we going to finish this wedding, or what?"

John-Michael looked around the church, at all the expectant faces. "It'd be a shame to waste all this."

"Yes, yes it would," Muffy agreed. They both looked at Sonya.

"Oh, sure, why not?"

She and John-Michael faced each other and held hands. "I, Sonya, take you, John-Michael, to be my lawfully wedded husband..." She spoke the vow with ease. Though she knew this ceremony wasn't legally binding, since she and John-Michael hadn't even applied for a license, they went through it all, anyway. They could accomplish the legal part at city hall next week. Meanwhile, they had a perfectly good wedding and reception at their disposal.

"I, John-Michael, take you, Sonya..." John-Michael didn't hesitate, either.

They didn't have rings, but Sonya at least took off the bogus ring Marvin had given her and handed it to Brenna. "Do something with this, will you?"

The priest squinted at them with rheumy eyes. "All done, then?" They nodded. "I now pronounce you husband and wife. And I believe I'll retire to the rectory and take some medicine."

Sonya and John-Michael kissed again, and the bewildered congregation applauded.

THE RECEPTION WAS DELAYED by an hour or so as the FBI questioned various members of the wedding party. The pricey photographer Muffy had hired ran around taking pictures of everything—he'd probably make a fortune selling them to the tabloids. But John-Michael didn't care.

His first week as a law enforcement officer, and he'd helped apprehend a fugitive felon. Granted, the take-down hadn't gone picture-perfect, and he'd had to rely on a bevy of blondes to do the dirty work, but he still felt supremely satisfied.

His minor professional success paled, however, when compared to what had happened in his personal life. He couldn't imagine why he had delayed so long in telling Sonya how he really felt about her. He'd accused her and her family and friends of being snobs, unable to accept a gardener's son into their midst, when really *he* was the one guilty of reverse snobbery.

Other than Tootsie Milford, everyone he'd talked to had treated him fine and wished him happiness. And Muffy...

"I'm so happy you and Sonya worked things out," Muffy said as she and John-Michael danced the Texas two-step to an easy-listening version of a Willie Nelson song, as performed by the Brent Warren Orchestra. "I hold myself partly to blame for the fact you two didn't get together long ago. I knew the attraction was there, and I discouraged it by making you responsible for Sonya. I knew you wouldn't betray my trust in you."

"You were right. But, shoot, Mrs. Patterson—"

"Muffy. Please call me Muffy. I'm your mother-in-law, and I might soon be your stepmother."

"Muffy, then. I don't think Sonya or I were ready for each other until now. We both had some things to work out."

"I know what you mean. It took a heart attack to make me see things clearly. Before that, Jock and I would have had difficulties."

"You'll still have difficulties," John-Michael reminded her.

"Oh, I know that." She glanced over at her friend Tootsie, who sat alone at a table nursing some sort of drink and looking as if she'd just bitten into a lemon. "Some of my friends—or the people I thought were friends—think I've gone insane. But that's all right. They'll come around when they realize this isn't some midlife-crisis fling. And when they get to know Jock. He's an exceptional man."

"That he is."

John-Michael and his father switched partners, and John-Michael found himself once again dancing with his "bride."

"This is the most fun wedding reception I've ever been to," Sonya said, brushing a butterfly off her face. "Despite the insects. I can't believe Mother actually got that cake with the butterflies inside when I told her not to."

"It was quite a moving moment when you removed the top from the cake and they all flew out."

"I'm sure everyone was very moved to see me

scream like a banshee and dive under the table. I'll get her back, though. Just wait until she and Jock get married. We'll see how she likes a wedding cake filled with flying toads."

"Where are you going to find flying toads?"

"I'll genetically engineer some."

"I thought you were a chemical engineer."

"I'll study up. Hey, I have a question for you. How do you feel about Greece?"

"I don't know. I've never been."

"Want to? Heath says they found two airline tickets tucked into Marvin's jacket pocket. Purchased with my credit card. Nonrefundable, but I can transfer Marvin's into your name."

"You mean a honeymoon?"

"Duh. Don't you think we deserve one, after all this?"

"But we're not even married. Not legally."

"Who cares? We'll fix that later."

John-Michael let himself fantasize for a few moments about a deserted beach, no reporters, rubbing suntan lotion on Sonya. Sonya in a bikini. "I'm there."

Sonya wrapped her arms around his neck. They stood still on the dance floor as other couples swirled around them. Another flurry of rose petals floated down around them. They'd been falling in light showers since the opening waltz, which Sonya and John-Michael had struggled through, stepping on each other's toes and murmuring "Sorry" and "Excuse me" every few seconds.

"Say it again, John-Mikey."

"I love you."

"And…?"

"I will never, ever let my stupid pride come between us again, even though you have more money than—"

"I don't. At my request, Mother is going to revoke my trust fund, and I've given her back all the credit cards. I'm going to make it on my own. Jock says you have the cutest house near Channelview. Can we live there, please?"

"It'll be quite a lifestyle change for you."

"I want it. I want us to live like normal people."

"We can live wherever you want. But only if you say it again, too."

"I love you."

"Hey, you two are so cross-eyed in love, you're making everyone else sick." It was Brenna. "Stop staring at him for two seconds, Sonya. You're needed elsewhere."

Sonya let herself be led away, shrugging helplessly to John-Michael. If it had been anyone else stealing his bride, he would have objected. But Brenna and Cindy were at least partially responsible for getting him and Sonya together. It wasn't until her time away with her two new friends that Sonya had started to reevaluate her life.

He supposed he should thank Marvin, too, and Muffy and Jock, all of whom had contributed. It was funny how events just came together sometimes. It was enough to make John-Michael wonder if there wasn't a cupid out there somewhere, feeling very pleased with himself.

Epilogue

"To The Blondes," said Brenna, and the three women hoisted their champagne glasses for about the dozenth time. Muffy knew how to pick good champagne, Sonya thought, as she swallowed a mouthful of the Dom Perignon.

"To friendship," said Cindy.

"To true love winning out over impossible obstacles," said Brenna."

"Hey, it's my turn," Sonya said. But now that Sonya had everyone's attention, she had a hard time coming up with something new. They'd toasted everyone and everything, from the orchestra to Muffy to the caterer who'd provided the incredible crab-stuffed mushrooms.

"Well?" Brenna looked at her expectantly.

"To Marvin," Sonya finally said, hoisting her champagne glass.

The other two stopped midtoast. "What?" they said together.

Sonya addressed Brenna. "If not for Marvin, you and Heath wouldn't have met." Then she looked at

Cindy. "And if not for Marvin, Luke wouldn't have had to rescue you from living on a leaky old boat. But most important, without Marvin, the three of us would never have met. You are the best friends any girl could want."

"Well, when you put it like that," Cindy said. "To Marvin."

Brenna joined in. "To Marvin, the ratfink."

Sonya giggled. "Can you imagine him in prison?"

Cindy arched one eyebrow. "Within a week, he'll probably con some guard into believing he's innocent and paying for his lawyer."

"Or helping him escape," Brenna said.

"Okay, that does it," Sonya said. "The three of us have to keep tabs on him. We have to make sure he gets prosecuted and remains behind bars."

"Hmm, I think that calls for monthly meetings," said Cindy.

"Oh, excellent!" Sonya raised her glass. "To monthly meetings. We may live in different cities, but we're going to stay best friends."

"To monthly Blonde reunions," Brenna agreed.

"ARE YOU SURE you're not too cold?" John-Michael asked for the third time. "You're shivering."

"I'm p-perfect," Sonya replied. Cold but happy. "I can see the rings around Saturn."

"Let me see." Brenna elbowed Sonya out of the way. "Oh, my gosh, it's so pretty! Maybe I should do some space-themed jewelry."

"Adam, sweetie, you want to look?" Cindy held her son up to the telescope, but he was too young to really understand or appreciate why, when it was freezing outside, they were all out in the middle of a field outside of Cottonwood, peering into a metal tube. "Oh, well, maybe in a few years."

Sonya had finally given John-Michael his thank-you present on their "wedding night," and he'd been so touched by the fact she remembered his youthful interest in stars and planets that he'd had to declare his undying love all over again—which suited Sonya fine.

They hadn't gone to Greece. John-Michael had been too new at his job and couldn't ask for vacation. But they'd managed to take a few days off a month later, and they were spending them in Cottonwood, far away from city lights and smog, where they could give the telescope a good breaking in. Cindy, Luke, Adam, Brenna and Heath had joined them for their official monthly Blonde Reunion. Thankfully, there hadn't been much to report about Marvin. He was behind bars, held without bail since he was a terrible flight risk, as prosecutors prepared their case against him.

Everyone took turns looking at Saturn. But Sonya's ears and toes were going numb.

"Who's ready for hot chocolate back at our house?" Cindy asked as if she'd read Sonya's mind, and no one objected to packing up the telescope for the night and focusing on a few less intellectual pursuits.

Around a popping fire, they all grew mellow as they sipped hot chocolate. Sonya cuddled with John-Michael in an oversize chair, while Cindy and Luke lounged on the sofa with Adam and the dog. Heath and Brenna sprawled on the floor on big pillows.

Sonya had never been so content as she was now, living her simpler life.

She had much to be grateful for. She had funny, loyal friends and a husband who adored her; her mother was almost fully recovered from her illness and had reclaimed her own love; and last week, she'd been offered a position with a small engineering firm that specialized in solar-energy applications. John-Michael had nearly passed out from the shock, but she'd tried not to take offense. After all, she'd surprised herself, too. Besides, surprising her husband once in a while wasn't all bad.

Her life was filled with almost too much good fortune for one woman to bear. Almost, but she would manage it.

MARRYING THE MARSHAL

Laura Marie Altom

U.S. Marshal Caleb Logue's new assignment is protecting the eight-year-old son he didn't know he had. Allie Hayworth wouldn't marry him nine years ago—claiming a lawman husband could make for an early widowhood—but she's darn well going to marry him now!

(HAR #1099)
On sale January 2006

Available wherever Harlequin books are sold.

If you loved
The Da Vinci Code,
Harlequin Blaze brings you
a continuity with just as many
twists and turns and,
of course, more unexpected
and red-hot romance.

**Get ready for The White Star continuity
coming January 2006.**

This modern-day hunt is like no other....

MINISERIES

National bestselling author
Janice Kay Johnson

Patton's Daughters

Featuring the first two novels in her
bestselling miniseries

The people of Elk Springs, Oregon, thought
Ed Patton was a good man, a good cop, a good
father. But his daughters knew the truth, and his
brutality drove them apart for years. Now it was
time for Renee and Meg Patton to reconcile…
and to let love back into their lives.

*"Janice Kay Johnson gives readers romance and
intrigue sure to please."*—*Romantic Times*

Available in January

Where love comes alive™

HARLEQUIN®

AMERICAN *Romance*®

You won't want to miss the fourth
installment of this beloved family saga!

A Texas Family Reunion
Judy Christenberry

Separated during childhood, five siblings from
the Lone Star state are destined to rediscover one
another, find true love and build a Texas-size
family legacy they can call their own....

REBECCA'S LITTLE SECRET (HAR #1033)
On sale September 2004

RACHEL'S COWBOY (HAR #1058)
On sale March 2005

A SOLDIER'S RETURN (HAR #1073)
On sale July 2005